EVERY DOOR IS LOCKED

Grey Liliy

BROKEN POCKET

Copyright © 2015 Grey Liliy

Published by Broken Pocket in 2015 in The United States of America.

ISBN-13: 978-1943161041
ISBN-10: 1943161046

Cover Design by Grey Liliy

For the Survival Horror Fans.
May there always be a message in your coffee and a
flashlight in your pocket.

CHAPTER 1

THE DOOR WAS locked.

Klawisz shook the brass knob, rattling the metal as he tugged and turned the handle. He continued his assault, switching up the shake of the knob with a hit to the wood with his shoulder. The door didn't budge an inch. Klawisz growled at the unwilling knob like a dog who'd seen a stranger in his yard as he gave it one last useless twist. He dropped his hand back to his waist, and kicked the bottom frame with the heel of his Chelsea boot. The hit echoed in the room, but the door barely rattled after the vicious strike.

He brushed back his black hair, slick and wet with sweat. Klawisz counted to ten, exhaling from the first count to the last. The front doors were locked. Klawisz rubbed his hand on the side of his neoprene peacoat, wiping away the perspiration on the coarse material. The back doors were also locked. He could say the same for the side doors, the hallway doors, the employee-only doors, and even the bathroom doors.

Every single door on the damned main floor was locked!

Klawisz twisted a key around in his fingers, the round metal disc on the keychain jingling as it turned. He held it up in the light of the nearest flickering wall lamp. The overhead lights were broken, useless and coated in the same blanket of dust as the rest of the lobby. It left the open room dim, but with the evening sun coming in through the tall windows, there was still enough light to see.

He ran his thumb over the metal of the keychain, digging his nail into the leftover indents. There had been a number on the fob at some point, but it had been scratched clean off with what looked like a knife blade. The criss-crossed scars were deep and vicious, leaving no sign of the prior number that had been there. Klawisz knew it was a room key, and while he knew for certain deep down in his gut that the room this key matched was his own, Klawisz couldn't remember the number or where his room was.

And he might never.

The hotel had thirty guest rooms per floor, thirteen above ground floors, and another four sub level floors below the lobby and entrance. Sure there were only guest rooms on eleven of those floors with the lobby on the first and a penthouse on the thirteenth, but that was still a hell of a lot of individual rooms he'd have to check to find this key's mate.

Klawisz rapped his knuckles on the main lobby door one last time, before turning away and heading toward the stairwell. He shoved the key into his front jean pocket, and scrunched his nose at the dust his feet kicked up as he crossed the lobby floor. Klawisz might as well start searching for his room when there was nothing else to do down here. It wasn't like he didn't have the time.

When he woke up in the middle of the hotel lobby floor with nothing but the clothes on his back and a room key, Klawisz took that as a cosmic hint that he should find the room that matched. Better to sleep on your own bed in your own room than on the lobby's dust-coated carpet.

It only made sense.

Klawisz brushed a cobweb out of the way as he reached for the stairwell door handle. He twisted it and—

It was locked.

The second time was the charm, and the door frame cracked from the strength of his second kick. The heavy wooden door burst inward toward the stairwell, and Klawisz licked the edge of his teeth. There was more than one way to open a locked door. He passed over the threshold, jumping over the shattered door remains. Klawisz walked under the landing to check the emergency door that led out to the street and found it locked as well. No amount of kicking, screaming or bruised shoulders budged that door.

Ignoring it for now, Klawisz skipped up the stairs two or three steps at a time toward the second floor. He was more interested in finding his room than a way out of the building, anyway. The desire to find the room that matched his key was too strong, easily overpowering the more logical choice of *getting out*. Another harsh kick smacked into the second story door, this time opening it wide in one hit.

"That has to be a fire code violation," Klawisz snorted to himself as he slid the stairwell door shut behind him with the back of his heel.

The long second floor hallway stretched out before him, dark and damp. The aged carpet was spotted with wear, dulled and flattened by time and too many shoes stomping over it. Only one or two of the multiple lights tacked up on the walls worked at a time, blinking on and off at random intervals. Their flickering was a distracting dance, changing the shadows in the hallway and making it hard to see too far down the corridor. Klawisz rubbed his cheek and breathed slowly through his nose.

The stench of mildew came from the carpets and the walls, rotten and wary.

The hotel building had been constructed in a single long strip, with a large square open area in the middle. Fifteen rooms were laid out along the two hallways on either side of the middle quad, which itself contained a vending area, an old elevator, and a small seating section with dusty couches and dead plants. The simple layout would make searching for his room easier. Systematic.

Klawisz looked to the side, and pulled the fire escape map out from its plastic housing next to the stairwell door. He reached into his inside coat pocket and pulled out a blue pen, his fingers brushing against the small leather journal that rested neatly in the pocket. Klawisz clicked the end of the pen and walked up to the first door on his right.

Klawisz crossed out the fifteenth room on his map with a large "X" through the door to match the other marks. Eight to one side of the hallway, and seven on the other: All locked, and all impervious to the frustrated kicks that followed when the key refused to open the door. The guest rooms had some sturdy doors in this place, that or something was jammed up against them on the other side. Not that he could think of a reason the guests should need to barricade themselves inside.

If there even were any other guests in this place.

He shoved the key and map back into his pocket as he entered the center square of the hotel. Klawisz rubbed his face, shifting his hand across his cheek until it rested on the back of his neck, and tried not to think about being alone. There had to be someone else in this place. Had to be. He'd even take the company of ghosts at this rate. Klawisz smacked his cheeks with both hands and concentrated on where he was. He was at the midpoint of the building, and that was progress.

The elevator loomed to his left, the iron gate blocking the empty shaft, its car on another floor somewhere. It was a dirt old hydraulic thing, with an iron cage that rattled and hummed as it dawdled up and down the shaft at a pace that would make snails look quick. It was a miracle of engineering that they got the thing to run to all seventeen floors in the hotel. Most elevators that ancient were only good for three or four floors at most. Too slow for anyone in a hurry.

Klawisz shivered with the gust of cold wind that came from the dark pit past its criss-crossed metal gate, and kept walking toward the vending machine across from it. Elevator to his back, his stomach rumbled, hungry for even the ancient things locked behind the glass. The inside was full of cobwebs and spiders, but the candy inside was wrapped.

"Chocolate never goes bad, right?" Klawisz said, pressing his hand against the glass to wipe away a streak of dust. To his luck, the vending machine was mechanical and looked like it still worked. Even though a few of the lights were technically working, which meant that power had to be on somewhere in the building, it didn't mean he trusted the electricity in this place to work as it should. Klawisz dug through his pockets for change, but finding none, he went for the next best thing: Vandalism.

Not like he'd seen anyone around this place who would care.

Taking a dead palm tree by the trunk, he swung it like a baseball bat and slammed the clay pot the plant called home into the glass. The pot cracked and the glass shattered. He dropped the tree back down to its original resting place next to the vending machine, ignoring the dirt that had spilled out from the pot's wound.

Klawisz fished out a few candy bars to stuff in his pockets, snatching as many of the dust-free treats as he could. He grabbed one more, and ripped open the wrapping with his teeth. The milky chocolate bloom that stared up at him was unsightly, but despite the white coating and rough texture, it still tasted fine. Granted, "fine" was a relative term, but the key here was the chocolate was edible. Klawisz held the treat between his teeth while he stuffed a few more bars of the treat into his inside coat pockets for the road.

The world outside taunted him through the two ceiling to floor windows that were on either side of the vending machines. He looked at the busy streets below, people going about their business in the evening light. He could see freedom just beyond that window, along with the parking lot for the hotel. He squinted, trying to remember which car might have been his. Klawisz put his open chocolate bar in his pocket and picked up the palm tree again.

He slammed the pot into the window as hard as he was able, grunting as he repeated the movement over and over.

Klawisz wheezed, breathing heavily after the tenth hit. Clay shards surrounded his feet, covered in clumps of old, moldy dirt. Klawisz kicked the mess off his boots and backed away from the window. He dropped the plant to the ground and ran his hands through his hair.

There wasn't so much as a scratch on the glass.

He pulled his chocolate out of his pocket, and watched the people down below. They opened doors freely in the buildings across the street, going in and out at will. No locked doors outside the hotel walls. Jealousy bubbled up inside his gut, coating his insides and making him nauseous. Klawisz turned away from the mocking glass before he felt completely sick, and turned his attention back to the center lobby.

Despite Klawisz's growing weariness and desire for a break, the dusty couches, that may have been maroon at one point, didn't look the least bit inviting. Rest could wait for when he found his room and collapsed in the bed he'd paid for. That in mind, Klawisz had no trouble continuing across the empty square, heading for the next set of fifteen rooms on the other side. There was another stairwell door at the other end, so once Klawisz was done here, he could bust in that door and continue up to the next floor.

He'd find his room in no time.

Klawisz bit down on the chocolate bar, and dug the key back out of his pocket. He slid the key into the lock and counted to ten in his head to calm himself. One room at a time. That's how it was going to go. The key fit in the door handle slot, but refused to turn. Klawisz pulled it out, and jammed his foot into the side of the door. It didn't budge. He crossed that room off his fire escape map, and turned behind to look at the room across the hallway.

The door looked like all of the others in the hotel, made of sturdy dark wood with a brass doorknob. The room number hung off the door in embossed individual number plaques that were chipped and rusted at the edges. They reminded Klawisz of motel door numbers more than a five-star hotel. The number plaques for this room read "02-17" and Klawisz made sure the door number matched the one on his fire escape map. The last thing he wanted to do was to skip or mark the wrong room after all his meticulous checking.

His key once again failed, but his kick didn't.

The door slammed open, smacking hard into the inner wall. Klawisz stared for a moment, blinking wide grey eyes at the open room. It wasn't his room, but maybe he could find something inside of it worth his while. Another person would be nice, or even a working phone. The overhead lights in the room were off, and Klawisz couldn't see past the first few feet into the doorway.

"Hello?" Klawisz asked, taking a step into the room. He knocked his knuckles against the door frame, trying to make sure he was known before sneaking up on someone taking a nap or some other scenario that would just be his luck. "Anyone home?"

The answer was yes.

CHAPTER 2

KLAWISZ SCRAMBLED AWAY from the open door and back into the hallway running as fast as his legs would carry him. His coat flared behind him, boots beating against the carpet with every desperate step to put distance between Klawisz and the thing in that room. Had to get to the stairwell. He needed to get to the stairwell right now, and his body had no qualms upping his adrenaline to get that extra boost of speed to make that happen.

The scratch of claws and pointed legs on the ground beneath the roar of a watery hiss kept Klawisz's pace at a full sprint as doors flew by him on either side. The wall lamps sparked as he passed, all of them turning on at once to fully illuminate Klawisz and the monster on his heels.

His feet slipped on the moldy carpet, nearly sending Klawisz tumbling to the ground. But his hands hit first, crawling forward to keep him from stopping or his knees from hitting the ground. He smacked into the wall, knocking loose a chunk of plaster before continuing his sprint.

A giant, warped Scorpion about the size of a horse screamed behind him, its tail high in the air and running fast in chase.

Klawisz felt its claws, pock-marked with gaping pores, snapping at his coat with every monstrous lunge. He searched his pockets for anything he could use as a weapon against it. The Scorpion continued screeching, getting closer and closer. Klawisz's legs burned, and the hallway seemed to stretch in front of him. It hadn't been this long before had it? Klawisz's hands clenched around the only thing he had in his pocket, and he turned, still running for the stairwell. He threw one of his wrapped chocolate bars into the center of the monster's multiple eyes.

It was about as effective as one might think.

It didn't even make the monster mad.

Klawisz slammed into the door at the end of the hallway, smacking his face into the wood. He took a second to reorient himself. When did the hallway end? Klawisz slapped his cheek, and decided not to look a gift horse in the mouth. If he was at the end, that meant the stairwell and freedom from the clicking legs that kept getting closer behind him. He pushed on the door but it was locked.

Klawisz was at the wrong end of the building.

This was the door he hadn't busted in yet.

Klawisz ducked when a claw went over his head, slamming into the door above his head. The wood splintered, raining about Klawisz's head. The creature hissed and screeched, swishing its tail around and legs scrambling underneath the twisting body. Klawisz ducked and dodged, managing to roll through the spindly, giant legs. The beast's claw remained trapped in the wood of the stairwell door, and Klawisz took his opportunity to sprint as fast as possible in the other direction.

New plan: Get to the open door!

He had just past by the elevator when he heard the crunch of a door ripped off its hinges. Klawisz looked over his shoulder, to see the Scorpion free itself and start his chase anew. Its eyes glowed red, bright enough to leave trails of wispy hot light in the air as the head moved.

Klawisz ran faster.

He crashed into the door at the end of the hallway, and pushed through it. He slammed it shut behind him and hiked it three to four steps at a time up the stairs. He was at the mid landing when the monster's claw slammed the door open and off its hinge. Klawisz clung to the iron railing, looking down at the snapping limb shoving its way through the passageway. The Scorpion's head wedged into the door, to be replaced by a snapping claw. It wriggled and shook, but remained in the hallway.

The door was too small.

"He can't fit," Klawisz said to himself. He laughed to himself in a relieved giggle, and hung on the handrail. He screamed down, "You can't fit, you son of a bitch!"

The beast hissed one last time, before scurrying away from the door. Klawisz relaxed, leaning on the railing and letting his arm hang over the edge. His chest heaved as he regained his breath. Klawisz rested his forehead against the cold metal, and let his hair fall over his eyes. That had been close. Too close. He slipped off the railing and sat down on the nearest step. Klawisz pulled a piece of chocolate out of his pocket and ripped off the wrapper with a vicious tug. Rationing could be damned as he took a bite from the sugar bloomed treat.

Klawisz found a sizable paperclip on the steps and used it to attach the third floor fire escape map on top of his second floor map. He rolled his shoulders and crossed his fingers that he found the room that matched his key on one of the other floors, because he had no desire to go back and visit Mr. Scorpion any time soon.

Speaking of the second floor guest, Klawisz took a second to pull out his leather notebook. He opened it up to a blank page, and drew a quick doodle of the second floor Scorpion. His drawing was no work of art, but the stick-figure like sketch was enough to get the point across. Klawisz wrote "2nd Floor" in large print next to the doodle and closed the book, sticking it back in his pocket.

If he was going to be finding more things like that on his journey, he might as well keep track of them.

After putting the book away, he turned his attention back to the third floor. He had rooms to check, and did just that. Ten minutes later, Klawisz crossed off the second locked room on the floor, and sighed looking down the hallway and the endless stretch of more doors.

There had to be a faster way to do this.

Klawisz leaned on the wall, ignoring the blinking light above his head. It was only the second floor he'd begun to check for his room, and he was already going out of his mind. Check with key, check with boot heel. Still locked? Move on. It was already repetitive and he wasn't even a third of the way done. Klawisz rubbed his face and sighed.

He shouldn't miss the giant Scorpion monster from the second floor.

But what other choice did he have? Checking doors with his key was the only idea he had. Klawisz lifted his foot as a cluster of cockroaches scurried out from a crack in the wall past him. They were each the size of his palm, clicking loudly. Klawisz jumped away from them and blinked, to see that the bugs were gone. No noise, no sign of them, and even the hole in the wall seemed to have been patched. Klawisz rubbed his eyes and counted to ten. He needed to clear his head. That's what he needed. Take a break, take stock of his surroundings and his options, and then get a new plan that found his room faster.

Klawisz folded his maps and pen, putting them away neatly into the inner pocket of his jacket. He walked down the hallway toward the seating area in the middle square across from the looming elevator. Dust or not, mocking windows or not, he fully intended to take a seat and rest for at least ten to fifteen minutes. Maybe he'd attack the vending machine again for more sustenance when he was done.

Maybe with his belly full and mind rested, Klawisz could remember what was even in his room, and why he needed to get in so badly. He plopped down onto the waiting area couch, a puff of dust filling the hair from the impact. He coughed and waved his hand in the air in front of his face to clear the dirt particles. When the lot of them had finally settled, Klawisz leaned back and ignored the dust transfer from the couch fabric to his jeans and coat.

It'd come out in the wash, hopefully.

Did the hotel have a laundry service? It had to have one. Probably somewhere on the ground floor near the lobby. Or down on a lower floor with the pool and locker rooms. Definitely wouldn't be near the restaurant or the gift shops. Too much foot traffic, and no one wanted to see stacks of dirty laundry when they were eating.

Then again, Klawisz held up his hand and rubbed the dust covered fingertips together, the hotel wasn't all that big on cleanliness was it? He chuckled to himself at his own joke, deciding the dust wasn't all that bad. It was just dirt.

Wasn't going to hurt him.

He leaned his head back, and listened to the hum of the wall lights burning brightly and inhaled the dust. It was all awful, but he was so tired. Klawisz's limbs felt like weights, and the couch was worn and comfortable.

Wouldn't take much to...

CHAPTER 3

"HELLO THERE!"

KLAWISZ leapt from his spot on the couch, startled by the spritely voice that had woken him. He held his hands up, fists at the ready and expecting another monster attack. Instead, he found a chipper man with glittering eyes a few inches from his nose. Klawisz breathed heavily, scrambling back to put more space between them. He watched the man in the hotel uniform carefully, trying hard not to stare at the literal sparkles that covered his pupils. "Who are you?"

"We don't usually allow sleeping in the common areas," the stranger said, swishing his finger back and forth. He leaned back from Klawisz, and smoothed down the front of his double breasted jacket. He straightened the cords hanging from his shoulders with a sense of pride. "If you need a nap, might I suggest relocating to your room?"

"Working on that," Klawisz said, tilting his head. The stranger's eyes still had that odd glitter to them in the center of his dark irises. He wore a pressed hotel uniform, and his nose sat crooked on his face, like someone had punched the guy and broken it. The man smiled all the same, amused and lively. Klawisz looked down the hallway both ways, and saw nothing but the standard dust and flickering lights. Where'd this joker come from? "Who are you again?"

"Ah, allow me to introduce myself," he said. The man pointed to his badge, and read the name there with an amused grin. "I'm Dashiell, and I am at your service, Mr. Wiśniowski."

"How'd you know my name?" Klawisz asked, frowning at the other man. His pushed his hands into his pockets, and squeezed them into fists. Just in case. "I don't remember telling you that."

"I make sure to know the names of all our important guests here," Dashiell said, smiling and without a hint of malice. "For just such an occasion where I find them napping in the hallways."

"And you work here?" Klawisz asked, pointing at the man's chest.

"Well, I suppose if you couldn't read my nametag, the uniform probably slipped your grasp, too," Dashiell sighed. He tugged on his jacket, straightening it out again and wiping off imaginary dust. Dashiell winked at Klawisz and grinned wide. "Yes, I work here. Specifically, I run the elevator. Which, by the way, is how I noticed you asleep on that couch."

"The elevator?" Klawisz asked, yet again, and looked over his shoulder at the closed gates in front of the plush red interior of a brand-new looking elevator car. It looked surreal surrounded by the dust and rusting metal of the gate on the landing and the worn cables holding it up. Klawisz pointed at the car, and avoided the operator's glittering eyes that laughed at him. "That elevator."

"The one and only," Dashiell said, sighing happily. He turned his head toward the car, and clutched both hands to his chest. Dashiell hummed, closing his eyes and giving Klawisz a few free moments from their odd gaze. "My home sweet home, it is. Isn't she a lovely thing? I take such good care of her."

"You do," Klawisz nodded, and looked around for any other mysterious people popping up out of nowhere. He wrapped his fingers around his room key in his pocket, glancing at Dashiell out of the corner of his eye. "Say, you wouldn't happen to know why the doors are locked on the main floor, would you?"

"I don't," Dashiell replied, tapping the edge of his chin with the tip of his finger. "But the Concierge on the first floor sure would. He knows anything and everything about this hotel, you see. It's his job."

"Then perhaps I should talk to him about where the hell my room is," Klawisz said holding up his key. He jingled the bottom clip, catching Dashiell's starry eyes. "Because I can't remember which one is mine, and the number's been scratched off this key."

"Oh, that is a shame, isn't it?" Dashiell said, tipping his hat. He snapped his fingers and bowed slightly as he waved his hand toward the elevator door. "So it's a good thing that I'm here and willing to deliver you to the first floor. He would most definitely know where your room is."

Klawisz looked at the elevator, taking in its spotless metal walls and dust free interior for two seconds. The rusted metal gates opened as if on cue, the rusted sound of screeching metal filled the area as they moved across the floor. It foiled the elevator car's inner gates, shining and polished, that soundlessly opened to welcome a new passenger. The warm walls of the car were inviting with their painted walls and gleaming hand rails. The entryway hung open, spread apart and waiting like a temptress.

It was too good.

Klawisz shook his head and held a hand up in rejection. "That's fine, I'll take the stairs."

Dashiell frowned, his eyes narrowing in a way that unsettled Klawisz's stomach. The stars dancing around his iris faded out, leaving a dark void. The look was gone in a blink, the stars returning just as fast. The elevator operator grinned at Klawisz with a knowing look, and tugged on his shoulder cords. Dashiell trot back to his elevator and stepped inside with a confident skip. He tipped his hat once again and said, "As you wish."

"I do," Klawisz said. As Dashiell took control of the vintage controls, the welcoming atmosphere fled from the area. The small confined space looked more dangerous and looming than ever. Dashiell wrapped his long fingers around the handle, humming quietly as he waited for just a second longer, hoping his possible passenger might happen to change his mind. Klawisz clutched his key in his hand, squeezing until the teeth of the key made an indent in his palm. "Definitely taking the stairs."

"Might as well while you can," Dashiell said as the rusted safety gate closed in front of his matching clean, rust-free inside gate. The contrast between the hotel floor and the elevator car once again confirmed his decision, and Klawisz took a few three steps away from the car. Dashiell slammed the control handle all the way up and the car lurched. "You'll be taking the elevator soon enough, I'm sure."

Klawisz watched as the elevator car moved upward toward higher floors and out of view. He reached into his pocket and pulled out another bar of chocolate for a bite. Klawisz saw stars with every blink, a mental parting gift from Dashiell, and shuttered as he turned away. Shoving the last of the chocolate bar in his mouth, Klawisz reached his hand in his pocket for another. Nervous eating. Just what he needed in this place. His hand came out of his pocket empty, and he sighed.

Klawisz was going to need to break another vending machine.

Dust covered the concierge desk located to the left of the check-in counter at the front of the lobby. Hidden in the shadows, Klawisz almost missed it walking by. The counter was spotless, free of anything but a layer of dust and no indicator that it had a specific purpose. Only the small sign that read "Concierge" tacked on the front side let Klawisz know he was in the right place. Faded posters of popular restaurants lined on the back wall behind a box marked "Outgoing Mail." The "Incoming Mail" case was empty, save for a small brown package with a white tag. Klawisz put his hands on the desk, drawing a small picture in the caked dust, and leaned up to look around and behind the counter.

He found the man's desk, but he had yet to find the Concierge himself.

A rat ran across the desktop, and Klawisz lifted his hands out of the way as it streaked past. The harmless creature disappeared over the end of the counter, leaving small footprints in the dust covered surface. Klawisz shook his head, ready to leave after yet another dead end when he spotted it: the bell.

A service bell had appeared on the desk top sometime between when Klawisz arrived and the rat ran past attempting to squash his fingers. The polished brash had been shined to the point Klawisz could see his face in the reflection. There was no possible way it had been there when he first walked up to the desk, let alone earlier when he first woke up in the lobby.

"What the hell?" Klawisz asked the dust, and reached his hand up. He smacked his palm down on the top, and hoped for the best.

A loud ring emitted throughout the entire lobby, an obnoxious sound that shuddered every surface. Klawisz covered his ears to block the noise, eyes scrunched shut as he hunched over. Echoes rang in his ears, rattling his brain and sending shivers down his spine. Klawisz breathed heavily through his nose, willing his heart to stop racing and the pain in his head to go away. After a moment, when everything seemed to still, he tested the sound around him by pulling a hand away from his ear.

"You rang?" A man asked, leaning his arm on the side of the counter. Klawisz stared at the stranger dressed in a dark, clean suit. He couldn't believe what he was seeing, which was impressive considering the Scorpion earlier and Mr. Stars-in-His-Eyes. The smug man ignored Klawisz's distress, resting his chin in his hand. He shrugged his shoulders in apathetic fashion, and said, "Though I already knew that you were going to."

The well dressed man teasing Klawisz wasn't the only new thing: The entire lobby from countertop to floor had transformed from filth to riches in the few seconds he had closed his eyes. Not a speck of dust was to be found anywhere, and Klawisz gaped openly at the polished marble floors under his feet and the sheer amount of gold trim and wealth that surrounded him.

Klawisz rubbed at the side of his eyes seeing the organized counter space, now complete with ledger books and various stacks of paper. A pen connected to the counter with a chain was off to the side next to the bell, and when Klawisz looked up, he noticed even the chandeliers had been cleaned until they sparkled under the now working lights. He leaned heavily on the counter, staring at the people he could now see. Men and women in uniform suits working behind the desks, bellboys carrying luggage, and toward the back he saw a maid pushing a cleaning cart as she headed toward a service door. Employees everywhere, but not another client. All of them were dressed in uniform or suits, just like the man now behind the counter.

None of that had been there before.

"Who are you?" Klawisz asked, rubbing his fingers together and targeting the closest one. "You weren't here before."

"Of course I was," the man said, scoffing and raising an eyebrow. He pointed straight at Klawisz's face and said deathly serious, "I'm always here. It's you who's going in and out, you know."

Klawisz squeezed the key in his pocket. "No, I don't."

"Of course you don't," the man continued, talking down to Klawisz like he were a toddler. The condescending tone of his voice irked Klawisz more than he'd like to admit, and he wondered if Dashiell would appreciate having a fellow employee that looked like he had a broken nose around this place. "Not everyone can know everything the way that I do. After all, I am the Concierge."

"Right," Klawisz said, wincing at what a horrible turn this was taking. He dragged his hand down his face as he took in the car salesman slick smile and the equally greasy hair grinning at him. The Concierge wore a nice suit, but everything else about him screamed slime. Klawisz was better off with the elevator operator and his bone-chilling ride. But, he was here for a reason, wasn't he? Klawisz reached into his pocket and pulled out his key, holding it up for the self-proclaimed know-it-all. "If that's true, then you can tell me what room this key goes to."

"Hmm," The Concierge said, plucking the key from Klawisz's hand quick as a mongoose. He turned it over back and forth between his skeletal hands and said, "Yes, well you're half right."

"Excuse me?" Klawisz asked, snatching his key back. He clutched it tightly behind his fist and slammed a hand on the desk. A bellboy behind him dropped a piece of luggage from the action, and quickly scrambled to pick it up. Klawisz focused on the Concierge. "What's that supposed to mean?"

The Concierge laced his fingers together on the counter top and leaned forward to destroy any sense of personal space between the two men. "It means that while I do know in fact to which room that key belongs, I can not tell you."

"What? Why not? The elevator operator said that you could!" Klawisz asked, grabbing the side of the countertop with both hands. He pressed the key on the counter, the fob hanging loosely over the edge. "I just want to go back to my room."

"I know you do," The Concierge soothed, reaching his hand across the counter and placing it over Klawisz's. His skin felt like ice, and a chill sent goosebumps down Klawisz's arm at the contact. The Concierge crooned, "And you'll get there. When you find it yourself."

"But until then, is there anything else I can help you with?" the Concierge offered, taking his hand back and shifting into a more formal pose behind the desk, his back straight and hands to himself. "I can easily get you a reservation with our Hotel Restaurant, five stars no less, on the house. What about a trip to our day spa? Massages make any evening more pleasant. Or perhaps I can interest you in any other service the hotel has to offer? I can handle all that and more, just say the word."

"I just want to go back to my room," Klawisz said, shoving his key back in his pocket. "I don't need anything else."

"I know," the Concierge said, slicking his hair back with his hand and staring at the countertop. "But I can't help you with that one."

"Well, thanks," Klawisz said, patting the countertop before turning away from the desk with his back to the Concierge. "I guess I'll just keep looking on my own for now."

"Please do. But don't forget, if you're ever in the mood for real food that isn't something you dug out of those broken down vending machines, do feel free to give me a ring any time," The Concierge said, snapping his fingers loudly afterwards. "I meant it when I said it was on the house."

When Klawisz turned back around, the desk had reverted to its original state, covered in dust and empty of any signs of life. Only the service bell remained, untouched and shining brightly in the corner. The room grew deathly quiet as Klawisz breathed, looking around for any sign of the man or anyone else he had seen earlier. Seeing nothing but the return of the broken down lobby and dust as it first appeared, he whistled.

His day just kept getting better and better.

CHAPTER 4

WHEN KLAWISZ ENTERED the stairwell, instead of going up, he
went down.

Searching rooms one by one wasn't getting Klawisz anywhere. And
now he knew that somewhere in this building were other people. Where?
Klawisz had no idea. They could be in another time, another space,
another universe, or just hiding out on another floor. He had no clue, but
he knew that they were here somewhere and that's all that mattered.
Though so far, he'd noticed that every person he'd seen had been a staff
member.

He made note of Dashiell and the Concierge in his notebook on the
way down the steps a few pages down from the Scorpion. If a doodle of
a little devil with crossed out eyes ended up next to the Concierge's name,
he felt he couldn't be blamed.

On a whim, Klawisz added a small mention of the bellboy he'd seen.
Out of everyone he'd seen running around in the background of the
lobby, that was the one that had stood out the most. Maybe he'd end up
seeing him again.

Shoving the notebook back in his pocket, he went back to the business
of exploration.

According to the fire safety map he'd snatched from the wall, beneath
the lobby were four sub levels, three of which were for guests and
contained all of the hotel services from the aforementioned restaurants
and day spas the Concierge had advertised. Klawisz hoped at least one of
those areas might have someone working here more helpful than the
Concierge turned out to be, or at least less unnerving than the elevator
operator.

It was a small hope, but it was a hope.

Klawisz kicked open the door to the first sub-level, the satisfying crunch of the broken lock music to his ears. Contrasting shining floors and well kept lighting filled the area, making the decrepit upstairs main floor and upper rooms look even worse by comparison. Every wall lamp had been polished, the tiles dirt free and clean down to the grout between the tiles. Klawisz caught a whiff of fried chicken from somewhere on the floor and couldn't stop his stomach from growling at the mouth watering scent.

It felt like stepping into a new world.

Grabbing the fire escape map, Klawisz started his walk down the hallway, passing by various shallow shops full of tourist trinkets and t-shirts. This floor supposedly kept the restaurants and shopping areas of the building, and as he passed by another room packed with overpriced sweets, Klawisz felt that description held true. He shoved the growing collection of maps into his inner coat pocket and whistled at the sparkling glass walls that protected the shops beyond. Everything from fine artwork, to shining jewelry with rocks that had to cost a fortune were held behind those walls once you got past the first few tourist traps.

He window shopped for a bit, but the high class goods reminded him that his wallet was empty. Aside from his identification and a faded photo of his grandmother, there was no cash or plastic to be found. It was hard to buy things when you didn't have any money. All the same, it was at least nice to look at what they had to keep his mind off upstairs and his lost room.

Klawisz tapped the glass as he passed by a rack of nice ties in the window display of a clothing store. He touched his top button right under his collar, wondering if the blue silk tie would match his shirt. Part of him wondered how he got dressed this morning without one, and his button-up shirt agreed. Klawisz dropped his hands and smacked his cheeks. He'd been down here too long. Nice clothes and matching outfits were the least of his worries when he still didn't know where his hotel room was.

His fingers crinkled against candy wrappers, and his stomach growled. His hunger wasn't as easily ignored as his need to be fashionable.

At the end of the long strip, past the elevator lobby full of decorative seating for waiting, Klawisz spotted a row of restaurants that filled the other half of the building. Three in total: A bar, a small family place finishing off the rest of one side, and the opposite side of the strip looked like a fancy, fine-dining place with chandeliers and the whole nine yards that ran the entire length of the hallway.

Both the family restaurant and the fine dining were guarded by locked glass doors, and little signs up that said "See Concierge for Reservations" up front and underlined at the entrances. It would be easy enough to break in, but why bother when there was an easier route? Klawisz headed for the bar, which thankfully had an archway instead of a door.

No breaking in required.

The floorboards creaked as he passed the threshold, revealing a dimly lit area behind a privacy curtain made of red velvet. While clean, the atmosphere was heavy with smoke and the kind of despair that attracted alcoholics like moths to a flame. Klawisz hesitated in the doorway, unsure if he should go in or not. Sure bars weren't always the happiest of places, but the upscale, expensive flatware and the wall of nothing but top-shelf was ominous in a place that gave him the same feeling as a back alley dive.

"Care for a drink, sir?" A woman asked from behind the bar.

Klawisz blinked, clutching tight to the leftover candy wrapper in his pocket. A young would who could barely have been eighteen, way too young to be serving those sort of drinks, waited behind the bar with an empty glass and a cleaning towel. Her smile was sweet, dressed in red lipstick that stood out like a sore thumb against the subtle make up covering the rest of her face. She wore a uniform made of a black pencil skirt, a blue button up shirt and a nice black vest.

Very professional.

"If you're intimidated by the selection," she said, tipping her head back to the expensive liquors, "My sister Julie next door is hoarding all the cheap stuff, but don't let that fool you. Her mixed drinks are magic, so it's definitely worth a shot if you're pinching pennies."

"I don't think I should be drinking," Klawisz said, his eyes scanning the back wall of the bar for a service door without much luck. If people were going to keep popping in and out of reality without explanation, being sober might be in his best interest. "Been one of those days."

"Don't I know those," she laughed. She drummed the bar top with her fingers, and bit the edge of her lip. She reached under the bar and pulled out an old fashioned seltzer bottle that would have looked at home in the 1930's. She shook it lightly, sending a new crop of bubbles all around the glass innards. "How about I make you a virgin spritzer on the house, since it's been 'one of those days', huh?"

Klawisz's stomach growled again, and he licked the back of his teeth. "Ah, I'm not sure."

"What if I threw in a snack? We've got amazing fried mozzarella," she said, leaning on the bar top. "You sound hungry."

"You're going to make me pay for that one," Klawisz said, shaking his head. He glanced around the empty room, taking in the vacant bar seats and tables. "And I'm a little short on cash."

She shrugged, popping a glass off a stack behind her. She twirled it in her hand before setting it on the counter. A bottle of pineapple juice and a small bowl of fruit appeared next the seltzer bottle, pulled out from under the counter or materialized on their own. Klawisz hadn't been paying that much attention to know which. The bartender licked her lips, almost smearing her lipstick and distracting him from the food. "I'll put it on your tab."

"I have a tab?" Klawisz asked, sitting down at the bar top. He crossed his arms on the counter, watching as she arranged her ingredients with care.

"Of course! All of our guests have one. It makes things far more convenient with it comes to billing," she said. As she spoke, a rather large monarch butterfly landed on a brandy bottle behind her. It flicked its wings twice, before disappearing as Klawisz blinked. He rubbed his eyes, as the girl squeezed a handful of lemon juice into the cup. "Why bother our patients with bill after bill when they can pay all at once?"

Klawisz caught her nametag as she leaned over to pour the pineapple juice in the glass with a couple spoonfuls of sugar. "Your name is Annie?"

"That's why it's on the tag," she said, shaking the seltzer bottle. She tilted the glass, dispensing the bubbly beverage into the juice. Annie popped a few cherries into the drink, splashing the fizzing concoction over the edge, and wedged a slice of pineapple on the side of the cup. She winked, and said, "And I am busy after work if that was your next question."

"No, not being that forward. Just thought it was a nice name," Klawisz said. "And thanks for the drink, but I think I'll pass on the cheese sticks."

"Suit yourself," Annie said. "And here you go sir!"

She passed over the chilled glass, and he counted to ten before taking a sip of the sparkling beverage. Fresh and crisp, the light tang of juice mixed well with the seltzer. Klawisz felt the smile grow on his face, relishing the delicious drink. He couldn't think of anything better after nothing but old chocolate to wet his appetite since he woke up. Klawisz leaned his head back to stretch out his neck, before taking another full gulp of the drink. "This is amazing, Annie."

"You ought to see some of the other drinks I can make," Annie said, putting away her supplies back in their hidden places under the counter. She dropped a small drink menu in front of Klawisz and he whistled at both the prices and the alcohol content. Annie giggled. "They'll knock you right off that bench."

"That's what I'm scared of," Klawisz said, sipping quietly.

"But just so you know," Annie said, tapping her fingers on the counter. Her spritely expression calmed, just enough to twist Klawisz's stomach. She patted the back of his hand, and leaned in conspiratorially. "If you ever do get hungry, go see the Concierge in the main lobby, okay? He'll get you into next door or across the way there no problem."

"So I've been told," Klawisz said. He nursed the sparkling beverage, almost afraid of when this one good thing of his would be gone. "But right now, I think I'm going to concentrate on finding my room."

Annie pressed her lips together and shrugged. "Let me know if you change your mind about the snack."

She was gone in a blink, leaving Klawisz alone once again. He heard the flap of soft wings behind his head, but dared not turn around. Klawisz clutched his glass tighter. The clinking of ice and the small fizzing bubbles were his only proof that she had ever been there.

Klawisz finished his drink too soon and found himself eager to get off that floor. Whether the mysterious butterfly or Annie was causing the itch to run, he didn't know. He left the bar and its concerns behind, and headed back for the staircase door he'd broken.

He skipped the next floor down, taking only a moment to break the stairwell door to get in and grab the map. Seeing it was nothing but a gym facility, spa, and a few full sized indoor pools, Klawisz figured it wasn't worth his time to keep exploring.

The rather large Checkered Beetle that had been sitting at the end of the hallway had also been a factor in his decision to move on.

Feeling no shame in avoiding confrontations with giant insects, he kept going down the stairs and kicked in the third sub level door and helped himself to the map on the wall upon finding the area clear or immediately harmful things.

The third level below the lobby opened into a long wide hallway that stretched from one end of the floor to the other much like the floors above it. On either side, were tall walls that held little signs every so often that read "Ballroom" followed by a number. Klawisz walked about twenty feet before finding himself at the first set of double doors. He reached for the door handle in the middle, and was not the least bit surprised to find it locked.

Klawisz ruffled the back of his hair with one hand, and twisted hard on the pull down handle. He shook the door, but it didn't budge. Klawisz backed up a foot, and jammed the heel of his foot into the lock in a motion now well practiced. The double doors crashed open, and Klawisz found thirty or so pairs of shocked eyes staring at him.

Packed with people, all of them half-transparent and dressed to the nines, the ballroom was quite occupied. Klawisz stood frozen in place, matching the gust of freezing air that came from the room. Filled with ghosts. The room was full of well dressed ghosts and cold air. Men in black suits and women in ball gowns that came to the floor in a multitude of colors. Soft music came from behind them, a floating string ensemble still playing a light waltz. One by one the fancy ghosts shrugged off the appearance of the intruder and went back to their mingling and dancing, happy to ignore his rude entrance.

Klawisz stood in the doorway, still paralyzed by the sight.

Half tempted to go inside and raid the buffet table, Klawisz clung to the door and tried not to openly lick his lips from the smell of roast beef. As a ghost walked by, laughing together with the girl on his arm, a layer of frost snaked its way up on Klawisz's jacket sleeve. His breath hung in the air in a thick fog, and he changed his mind about going into the room. Klawisz grabbed the handle again to pull the doors shut before even more of the frigid air could sneak out of the room. He held his hands up, waiting for the door to slide open again with the faulty lock, but blew out a warm breath when the door remained snug in place. He rubbed the back of his neck and shoved his hands in his pockets, trying to forget the sight of the buffet table on the other end of the room and the growing growl of his stomach.

It was probably rotten.

Since when did ghosts need to eat?

Klawisz looked for a vending machine, but saw none on this floor. That could be for the best, since he might not be able to get away with breaking anything down here. It worked out well enough on the upper floors since everything was already in disrepair, but down here everything still looked prim and polished. Not to mention the employees popping in and out when he least expected them had already doubled since stepping food in the lobby.

After one last desperate search for food on his person, he found the last of his stolen goods from the vending machine hidden away and squashed in his peacoat pocket. He wasted no time in digging it out, and ripped open the wrapper with the edge of his teeth. Klawisz huffed at the bloomed chocolate, trying to ignore the sight of the roast beef and fresh rolls he'd seen on the buffet tables. His stomach growled all the same, and he bit into the bar. As he munched, Klawisz stood in the empty hallway and jotted down a few notes about Annie and the Ghosts in his notebook as he considered his options.

To check another room, or not to check another room?

The first set of double doors for the next ballroom were also locked. Klawisz twisted the handle and used his shoulder to bust the door open this time, hoping to keep hold and stop from making his entrance too dynamic should this room also be filled with dancing specters.

It opened with a harsh click, the lock snapping, and Klawisz stuck his head through the crack in the door.

Empty.

Gently pushing the wide double doors open with both hands, he went inside. Klawisz' footsteps echoed in the empty room, making it seem larger than it was. Looking around the giant area with its decorated tile floors and golden chandeliers hanging from the ceiling, Klawisz found himself spinning around trying to take everything in. Decorated lamps hung on the walls, and everything from the crown molding on the walls to the raised stage platform in the corner looked expensive.

The crystal jingle of a chandelier to his left caught his attention, and Klawisz looked up. His eyes widened, and he suddenly wished for the frostbitten dancers of next door. The Spider that clung to the web on the ceiling was massive, dwarfing the Scorpion that had caused so much trouble on the second floor. Slick, the smooth legs of the arachnid expertly placed silvery threads around the chandelier, creating an intricate web.

Brilliant yellows decorated the black Spider's back in splotches of color, and Klawisz found himself almost mesmerized as the creature worked. Like the Beetle before, he decided to leave well enough alone and get out while the getting was good. Ignored by the Spider, Klawisz backed out of the room and gently pulled the doors shut.

Reminding himself to breath, Klawisz checked the rooms across the hallway with equal care. Thankfully, there were no more giant Insects to give him heart attacks or attempt to draw in his journal. He found the rest of the ballrooms full of dust and used as storage for spare tables and chairs. No food, no giant insects, and no people—ghost or otherwise. He left footprints in the dust as he entered the dark area, listening for any sign of life he'd missed.

Klawisz played with the room key in his pocket, standing in the center of the cramped room.

Another dead end.

Klawisz kicked in the door on the lowest floor: The equipment rooms.

Snatching the fire map off the wall, he tacked it to the growing stack and genuinely considered breaking into the gift shop and getting a proper folder for them. Instead, he kept to the moment at hand and looked over the floor room layout. Unlike the many floors above, this one contained the nitty gritty inner workings of the building resulting in a maze of small rooms and corridors.

Electrical rooms with their giant buzzing switch boards, Mechanical rooms filled with pumps and generators, and even an elevator room that kept that creepy lift going up and down; it was all on this floor. Klawisz clicked his tongue as he started across the concrete floor, fairly certain that most of this stuff shouldn't be below ground, but who really followed building codes these days?

He turned at the first corner he came across, the layout down here resembled a mass of squares within squares. The lowest basement floor wasn't constricted by the long hallway and center square of the upper floors, and was instead a massive space with its own unique layouts. While it was different, Klawisz appreciated that the layout was at least straightforward. Four major hallways were surrounded by rooms, with an offshoot surrounded by its own rooms on each corner to reach the ends of the building. Klawisz tested the first door he came across with a wriggle of the handle.

Locked.

Klawisz kicked it in, proud at the ease of which yet another door caved to his foot. Not that it was a skill he felt like he should have, but it was, and he'd be proud of it if he wanted.

That could have been the hunger talking.

"What'd you do that for?" A man yelled from the other side, backing away from the attacking door.

A voice that wasn't coming from the exhaustion and hunger.

"Ah, sorry!" Klawisz said, holding his hands in front of him. He glanced down either side of the hallway looking for someone who might come running from the exchange. No one did. Klawisz offered, "Didn't realize anyone was down here."

Old and wrinkled, the elderly man's face was worn like old leather and threatened to fall off on the edges. Both of his eyes had gone white with cataract, but his gaze burned intensely enough that Klawisz had a feeling his vision was just fine. He reached over and grabbed a cane, using it to stand up. A jingling caught Klawisz's attention, and he immediately locked eyes on the keyring at his belt line. Thirty or forty keys, of all shapes, sizes and metal colors, clattered together as he stood.

Now that would be handy in a building where every door was locked.

"Guests shouldn't be down here," the old man said. Klawisz looked past his shoulder and spotted a mop sink and a shelf full of cleaning supplies. Janitor's closet. As the old man got closer, Klawisz caught sight of a name tag that merely read "Janitor" and nothing else. The old man grabbed Klawisz's arm, his fingers twisting into the fabric of his sleeve. "Who let you in? Those doors should be locked!"

"Trust me," Klawisz said, scratching the back of his neck with his free hand. He winced under the Janitor's grip and hissed with the man kept hold only to squeeze tighter. Klawisz pushed at the wrinkled fingers, hoping to dislodge the hand before it cut off his circulation or worse. "They are."

"Crazy kids, going where they shouldn't be," The old man muttered to himself. He left the small janitor's closet, dragging Klawisz behind him with the strength of a body builder. Klawisz tripped as he was yanked, barely catching himself from hitting the floor, and the old man continued his ramblings while his iron grip on Klawisz never faltered. "Shouldn't be down here. It's dangerous. Who knows what limbs they'd lose or monsters they'll run into. Idiots all of them. Just looking for danger."

"Dangerous?" Klawisz asked, looking behind at all the unexplored rooms. "Monsters? Like that Scorpion on the second floor or the Spider in the ballroom?"

"Dangerous," the Janitor confirmed, ignoring the second question. He dragged Klawisz down through the dark corridors and stopped at the elevator shaft in the middle of the building. Klawisz watched as he jammed his palm on the Elevator call switch. "Let's just get you back upstairs, shall we?"

The elevator dropped to the final floor with a clang, and no matter how much Klawisz struggled, the Janitor refused to release his arm. Sheer determination had to be powering the old man, as there was no muscle to be found. All the same, his bony fingers dug into Klawisz's flesh even harder to prevent his fidgeting when Dashiell's smiling face came into view.

His pupils still held a universe of stars, that had spread into the dark blue of his iris. Dashiell's eyes locked with Klawisz's gaze, and everything around them froze. As poetic as having stars in one's eyes sounded, when it came to Dashiell, it seemed more like dead space than anything so romantic. Dashiell's stars were bright lights in an infinite void that made Klawsiz's insides twist and his nerves flutter.

Klawisz rubbed his eyes; that was most definitely the hunger talking.

"Had a feeling I'd be seeing you again, Mr. Wiśniowski," Dashiell said. He stepped aside as the Janitor shoved Klawisz past the two gates and into the plush elevator car. Dashiell shut the gate with a deafening *clang* and smiled brightly. "Going up?"

CHAPTER 5

"YOU REALLY OUGHT to be more careful with where you disappear to," Dashiell said, whistling right after his sentence. He kept one hand on the elevator control as the machine climbed at the pace of a snail to the upper floors. Dashiell rubbed the side of his crooked nose, perfectly at ease as the car rattled, moving about an inch a minute. "Never know what you'll find in this place."

Klawisz grunted and watched the floor number lights at the top of the car. The sounds of the outside shaft were amplified tenfold in the car, from the slight screech of the old cord pulling their weight up, to the car tapping lightly against the wall every so often. The decorations and finery placed with care inside the car were failing distractions when every rattle reminded Klawisz of the elevator's age. His death grip on the side inner railing could have given the Janitor a run for his money.

Klawisz kept his back to the wall, holding himself up with his hips as his knees shook. "Drop me off on the next floor."

"You sure I can't drop you off at the lobby instead?" Dashiell asked. He rubbed his hand in a circle over his belly with a condescending, knowing smile. His eyes twinkled as well, and this time it wasn't from the blasted stars as the man made fun of him. Klawisz ignored his stomach growling as the man smirked. "I imagine you're getting awfully hungry right about now, and the Concierge has been dying to make an appointment for you."

"He doesn't have any other guests he can bother?" Klawisz asked, already planning to make a break for the stairs and a floor with a vending machine the second he was out of this death trap elevator. "Someone who wants his attention?"

"Each and every guest receives the utmost care at this establishment," Dashiell said. He tapped the side of his face, just under a star-filled eye. Klawisz looked away from him. Dashiell's voice continued, soft and reassuring. "Even you."

Klawisz kept his back plastered to the wall, and eyes locked on a spot just to the operator's right. Keep him in sight without looking directly at him. Good plan. He willed the elevator to get to its destination already. Klawisz exhaled slowly. "Just drop me off at the ballroom floor. I'll get off there."

"I'm afraid I can't do that," Dashiell said, sighing heavily. He clicked his tongue as the car continued its sluggish, jerky ride up the side of the building. "Seems you caused quite the stir during one of our top client's special events. They've asked you not return."

"Didn't realize there was anyone down there," Klawisz said, licking the back of his teeth. *Or that I caused a stir, since they seemed so keen on ignoring me,* Klawisz thought to himself. Dashiell kept smiling and Klawisz twisted his hand on the railing. The car jerked and he bit his lip as his stomach tried to cave in on itself. Klawisz stared at the tips of his boots; concentrated on his breathing. "Gym floor's good enough, then. Maybe I'll check out the pool."

"Sure you don't want to go to the lobby?" Dashiell asked, his bright smile faltering for a second. His eyes flicked to the side and back. Klawisz could practically see his brain whirling with words he wanted to say, but didn't for some reason. Dashiell's smile continued to strain, an odd concern showing through the expression. "There really isn't much on the lower floors for you without the Concierge's assistance."

"I can get to the lobby from the stairs," Klawisz said. He twisted his hands around the hand rails and breathed harder. He wiped sweat from his brow, and shook his head to focus. "Better for me. Exercise."

"You're not looking so well," Dashiell said.

"I'm fine," Klawisz said. The room spun and he leaned his shoulder against the wall. Klawisz held the side of his head, and licked the side of his lip. The floor twisted under his feet, and he shook his head. "Just drop me off on the nearest floor."

"You're about to drop right now," Dashiell said, voice distant and muffled, almost like he was talking through a wad of cotton.

Klawisz focused on a paisley in the print on the floor. He squeezed his fingers in his hair and shook his head. The patterned swirl looked closer and closer the longer he stared at it. Too close. Klawisz thumped on the floor, rolling on his back. He stared at the ceiling, as the elevator spun.

Dashiell wasn't wrong.

Klawisz woke to a chandelier hanging over his head.

The sparkling gold shone brightly over head, showing off glittering surfaces. It almost hurt to look at the shining light fixture, so clean and tidy against the clean white tiles of the ceiling. His arms hung over the armrests of the lobby chair, and his back was slumped into the seat like he'd been dropped there. Klawisz pulled his arms up and covered his eyes, blocking out the chandelier light. He scrubbed up and down, willing himself to wake up.

As consciousness returned, Klawisz dared to drop his head and look around the dust-free lobby. He blocked out the sounds of bells ringing and people running about in the background of what should have been an empty floor.

A silent bellboy stood a safe distance away, about ten feet, staring. Unlike the rest of the employees running about, this one had his attention locked onto Klawisz. His stare was intense, and the boy fidgeted in place, unsure if he was supposed to be doing something. Looking familiar, Klawisz recognized the bellboy as the one who'd dropped the luggage earlier. His uniform matched Dashiell's, equally clean and pressed. Klawisz ignored him for the moment.

The Concierge smiling at him from the desk demanded more attention.

Klawisz held his face in the side of his hand, the world righting itself from his dizzy fall in the elevator. Or at least he had been in the elevator. But now he was in the lobby? He remembered seeing the floor get closer, and Dashiell moving, but not much after that. Had he passed out? Klawisz groaned, rubbing between his eyes. He was hungry and tired, and really had no desire to deal with all this.

All he wanted was to find his room.

Why was that so much to ask?

"Dear Dashiell rang the bell for you," the Concierge said lightly from behind his desk. He held up a small slip of paper, a coy smile climbing on his face. The sleazy, slick grin made Klawisz want to punch him all over again. The Concierge didn't seem to notice Klawisz's inner hostility and continued on smugly, "Might I interest you in that restaurant reservation now?"

"I'll pass," Klawisz said, even as his stomach growled and roared.

"Come now, you're hungry," The Concierge continued. "I know that you are. Just come here and make a quick little reservation and get something to eat."

"Said I'll pass," Klawisz repeated. The bellboy kept watching him, his fingers twitching as if to make a move. He looked at the Concierge and back to Klawisz, but didn't move. "And I'm going to say the same thing over and over. I don't want your reservation."

Klawisz pushed out of the chair and walked straight past the waiting bellboy before the kid could grab his arm. He made straight for the broken stair door, and the hope of getting back to the bedrooms. He didn't need dinner, he needed his room.

The key burned a hole in his pocket, just begging to be used.

That had to come first.

"You're going to want that meal sooner or later!" The Concierge shouted from the counter. A layer of vitriol coated his voice, bringing forth an almost hiss to his declaration. Klawisz jumped as he smacked the countertop, the sound echoing in the lobby and stilling all of the phantom employees running about. "Dashiell won't always be there to drag you back here when you pass out next time!"

Klawisz pushed open the still broken stairwell door and left the lobby behind. His stomach growled again, echoing around the concrete steps. Klawisz ignored it and started climbing.

He'd break into another vending machine.

CHAPTER 6

THE THIRD FLOOR had been a bust, in every sense of the word.

If it wasn't bad enough that the vending machines had been completely empty of anything Klawisz could loot out of them, he also hadn't found anything on the rest of the floor. Save for an irregularly large swarm of one inch tall black ants, that is. They were their own sort of monster, with legs sharpened to points instead of he usual joints. Klawisz could hear each and every little prick of the carpet as they moved, the sound a harsh rustling and rip of fabric. He made sure to jot down notes about the ants using large print in his notebook so he wouldn't forget about them later.

If that were even possible.

The ants thankfully ignored Klawisz as he traveled the hallways, his speed impeded by the need to check his feet every few steps to make sure he hadn't squashed one on accident and incurred their wrath. The threat of tiny pinpricks crawling up his legs and face was not nearly as worrying as the thought of them digging their sharp pincers into flesh and stinging him. Klawisz had seen a swarm of ants devour a bird in his grandmother's yard when he was younger. He knew what those little monsters were capable of, even when they were a quarter of the size of the ones crawling around his feet. Thankfully, they kept close to the center of the corridor, which made avoiding them a tad easier, even as the sound of their legs scurrying about sent chills up his back.

Ants aside, after thirty rooms checked, Klawisz found all of the guest rooms locked and none of them a match for his key. Klawisz managed to break into one empty room to catch a quick cat nap on a dust covered mattress, however, and that managed to be the highlight of his day.

He wasn't sure for how long he actually slept in the borrowed room, but he woke up as hungry as ever. The extra boost of energy he'd gotten from sleep did little to ease his aching stomach, but it did motivate him to get moving. Klawisz didn't know how, but he just knew there'd be food and a clean bed waiting in his room.

Klawisz stared at the room key in his palm, the scratched number tag falling just off the side of his palm.

He just knew it.

Now if only Klawisz could find the damned place. He climbed the stairs, hauling himself up with the railing and skipping steps as he went. Each footstep echoed in the empty stairwell, the concrete stairs old and worn beneath him. Their decay increased as he went further up the side corridor, and he prayed that this was the worst of it or he'd be stuck with the elevator later.

"This floor better have a vending machine," Klawisz said, kicking open the stairwell door to the fourth floor. He grabbed the fire escape map on instinct and stuck his key into the first door on his right. He licked his teeth as it refused to budge.

Locked.

Klawisz kicked the door, and marked a large "X" over the room on his map. He moved onto the next door, ignoring the empty feeling in his stomach and the growing desperation with every checked room.

The next door didn't match his key either, but he was able to kick this one open. Klawisz marked a circle around the room on the map, and shoved it all back into his pocket. He opened the door fully, careful and slow in case something or someone were inside.

The smell of dust and liquor slammed into him, like walking straight into a wall. Klawisz stepped inside covering his mouth and nose with his palm, and flicked the light switch on the wall. His nose wrinkled at the broken booze bottles everywhere. Spilled and knocked on their sides, broken glass and stains covered near every surface.

His boots crunched on the broken glass as wandered around the room, happy that it at least seemed free of insects. Klawisz kept his eyes open for anything that could be useful, like forgotten snacks or a baseball bat. He found mostly more broken bottles and trashed furniture. A half-used pack of cigarettes and a lighter that Klawisz shoved in his pocket being the exception to that "mostly."

Klawisz opened the closet. He picked up the broken clothes iron that had fallen to the floor and moved it out of the way. One of the hotel provided safes sat in its proper place in the bottom corner of the closet. The door was closed, and Klawisz hummed. The little light on the front blinked "Locked" and that was no surprise. The keypad next to it blinked, and Klawisz shrugged.

He typed in the code 1-2-3-4 and laughed when the door unlocked.

"Need to be more creative than that, buddy," Klawisz said as he pulled open the safe door with a happy whistle that dissolved into an awed whistle as he took in the contents. "Should have been much more creative."

A revolver sat on the top shelf of the safe, polished and clean.

Klawisz wrapped his hand around the handle and pulled the weapon from the small safe. He opened the cylinder and counted six chambers, but only five bullets were loaded. Klawisz put the gun in his outer coat pocket and zipped up the side. Using it wasn't quite on his agenda yet, but with monsters downstairs and all the other untrustworthy folks in the building, he'd rather have it on him than off him.

He pushed a broken bottle aside as he looked around the rest of the room. There'd been no ammunition in the safe, but that didn't mean there might not be any in the side table drawers. You were supposed to store ammo and guns apart from either other, anyway. Klawisz opened each one, on both sides of the bed, but didn't find anything but a spare copy of the *Bible* and another pack of cigarettes. He slammed the last dresser door shut, and rubbed the back of his neck.

Around the bed, though, Klawisz did find an unharmed, small and flat bottle of brandy on the floor next to the bed. He picked it up and tapped the top with his fingers when he saw the seal still firmly intact on the top. That was definitely something he could use later when he got desperate enough. Maybe even before that point. Klawisz shoved the small bottle into his coat pocket next to his leather and used the side table to pull himself up from the ground.

He wondered if Annie would be mad if he showed up with his own booze and asked for those cheese sticks.

As he brushed off his coat, Klawisz saw something past the lamp on the side table: Writing on the wall, written in what looked to be dried blood that was already turning brown with age. Someone had listed the combination from the lockbox on the wall in large, shaky numbers: 1-2-3-4.

"Thanks, buddy," Klawisz said, laughing. His throat and stomach hurt from the absurdness of it all, laughing so hard he couldn't breathe. After he took a moment to settle down, Klawisz rapped his knuckles on the top of the side table, before wiping a tear out of the side of his eye. "But I had it covered."

Leaving the booze room behind, new gun in his outer coat pocket and a bottle of brandy snug and tucked away in an inside pocket, Klawisz checked the next door: Locked. Key failed. Kick failed.

Move onto the next.

Klawisz cleared one entire corridor this way, all of the room doors made of steel it seemed. Out of fifteen rooms he could only break into one of them. He was either losing his touch with his kick, or the doors were reinforced somehow on the other side. Like they didn't want Klawisz to get in. He laughed at the absurdity (and more terrifying truth) of sentient rooms, and made his way to the center lobby.

The empty elevator shaft loomed like always, with rusted metal gates and dirt covered floors. He could see the wires moving as the elevator moved on other floors and shivered at the screeching sound. Klawisz turned away from the uninviting scene and glanced toward the vending machines and—

There were no vending machines.

The two floor to ceiling windows were in their proper place, but instead of the standard two vending machines was a door.

Klawisz glanced out the window and looked to the side to where the doorway was located. The parking lot lights allowed him to see a little in the night, but it was still difficult to make out the details in the dark. He smashed his cheek against the glass but no matter which direction he looked, he could only see the brick wall of the building's exterior where the doorway was located. Risking it, Klawisz took hold of the handle and twisted. Locked. Klawisz shook the door by the handle, but with the chance there might be nothing on the other side but a drop, he didn't dare kick it in yet. The entire frame rattled, but the door lock didn't want to break.

He checked the other side of the door from the window again, still seeing nothing but a long drop down from the outside.

The door loomed over him, promising something beyond. Light

peeked out from the gap between the door and the floor, far too bright to be from the parking lot.

Klawisz took a closer look at the door and focused on the hinge. This door opened in toward himself instead of out like the rest of the doors, and that made things a little more difficult. Klawisz grabbed the handle and braced his foot on the wall next to the frame. He grunted and yanked back as hard as he could. Klawisz shifted his hold and yanked again, shaking the entire door on its hinge.

The door didn't open.

Not to be deterred, Klawisz marked the door on his map and headed down the hallway. He'd be back for that as soon as he got something he could pry the door open with. Something was important with that doorway. He just knew it.

Klawisz needed a crowbar.

Where would he get one of those? He shook his head and continued to trot down the hallway. The next room down failed both lock and kick tests, so Klawisz moved onto the next. Four doors down, he hit a jackpot and the door kicked open. Klawisz grinned, pushing the door open with the back of his hand.

The smile immediately fell from his face when the smell accosted him. He covered his nose with his hand and stumbled back into the hallway coughing. Klawisz yanked a handkerchief out of his pocket and covered the lower half of his face, breathing through the thick fabric. He left the door looming open, and debated the pros and cons of going back inside. He preferred the stench of alcohol to the rotten sweetness inside that room. Klawisz watched the door. It swung open further on its own, just an inch or so. Inviting him in.

Breathing heavily through his mouth over his nose, Klawisz inched back toward the room. The smell wormed its way through his handkerchief, but he squashed the urge to vomit.

Sprawled out on the bed was the source of the odor: a dead body, its toothy mouth hanging open and tongue long wasted away. The poor soul had scraps of hair still hanging on his head, and the clothes looked worn and old. Blue jeans and a plaid shirt, ripped open across the side exposing green skin. Despite half of him rotted away, the body still looked rather peaceful with one hand resting across his chest. The other hand was clenched tight to a crowbar near his waist.

A perfect, shining crowbar.

"What're the odds of that?" Klawisz said, whistling. He walked around the edge of the bed and grabbed the crowbar end with his free hand. Klawisz said, "Sorry, buddy, but I kinda need this."

He yanked hard, but neither the arm nor the crowbar would move. It was like trying to tug the sword out of the stone when your name wasn't "Arthur." Klawisz grunted and shoved his handkerchief in his pocket, coughing for a moment as the smell renewed itself, and grabbed the crowbar with both hands.

Bracing his foot on the side of the bed, Klawisz tugged again. He managed to lift the body a few inches off the bed, before loosing his grip and falling back. He slammed into the floor and groaned as the body settled back into place, still holding the crowbar.

Klawisz rubbed the back of his head and reached for something to pull himself up with. His fingers found the side table, and found themselves wrapping around something soft on the surface of the wood top. Klawisz tugged it down, finding himself staring at a leather journal that looked quite a bit like his own.

He opened the little book, and flipped through a few pages of writing. Most were quick entries that were comprised of lists: Which doors he'd tried to open, numbers in seemingly random orders, and something about a restaurant menu. Klawisz continued flipping through until he found the last entry:

May 8
Still lost. Still can't find my room.
Nothing makes sense any more.
Wish I still had my booze.

Klawisz shut the book and shoved the leather in his pocket with his own, and his fingers brushed against the brandy bottle he'd gotten from the second room on this floor. He pulled it out of his pocket and shook the liquid around inside.

The body moved.

CHAPTER 7

KLAWISZ DIDN'T MOVE, too busy staring at the hand that had lifted up to even think of doing anything else. The outstretched arm, the only thing moving on the corpse, resembled a marionette's arm controlled by a poor puppeteer as it groped through the air toward the bottle of brandy in Klawisz's hand. The wrist bent as if there were a string tied around it, flopping the palm of the hand up and down. Testing, he stuck his own arm out to wave above it, seeing if there maybe was a string there and someone was trying to pull the wool over his eyes.

He didn't find a string, and the corpse's hand continued to stretch toward its goal. The fingers flexed in and out, over and over as they swayed toward the bottle just out of reach. Klawisz lifted the small bottle higher, and the hand followed. No matter which way he pulled the bottle, the arm followed with the same marionette-like motion. Klawisz glanced at the bottle and back at the corpse.

"This is my booze," Klawisz said, pulling the bottle back to his chest. The hand slammed into the bedspread and came back up with a new vengeance, still reaching for the brandy. Klawisz nearly smacked the hand away, but he still had no desire to touch it. "You can't have it."

The hand continued to shake the bed and the body, jostling the crow bar.

Klawisz bit the side of his lip and slowly undid the cap of the brandy. He took a tiny sip of it, enjoying the burn as it went down his throat. Klawisz watched the hand tremble, before forming a fist and shaking in jealousy.

"Tell you what, though," Klawisz said, feeling more amused than scared now that he'd seen that only the arm moved. He pretended to take another drink, stopping when the hand opened up and grabbed desperately at the air toward his bottle. "I'll give you a swig if you give me that crowbar."

The hand hung in the air, perfectly still, for a few moments.

It dropped to the mattress like its invisible puppeteer had dropped the strings. With a sickening crunch as the jaw moved, the body's mouth opened wide. Klawisz slid to the bed, his shoulders tense and eyes locked onto the hand. He pulled off the brandy cap and upturned the bottle over the corpse's mouth. A slosh of the liquor went down the thing's throat, with a dribble of it running down the sides of its decaying teeth.

Klawisz jumped back when the second arm let go of the crowbar and it clattered to the floor with a heavy thunk.

He looked between the still body and the crowbar. Klawisz screwed the cap back onto the bottle and placed it in his inner pocket next to the dead man's journal. The corpse didn't move. Keeping his eyes on the contented figure on the bed, Klawisz slowly knelt to pick up the crowbar. His hand searched the ground until his fingers wrapped around the cold iron of the metal bar. Klawisz backed away, starting crouched and straightening as he approached the door.

The body on the bed stayed still.

Klawisz looked at the crowbar in his hand, and bit the edge of his lip. He hit it against his palm once or twice, taking in the weight and sturdiness of the device. He looked back at the body on the bed and did a side salute from his head. "Thanks, buddy."

He shut the door behind him as he left the room, crowbar in his grip. He stood in the empty hallway, one hand around the crowbar and the other in his pocket. Klawisz whistled to the air and said, "Well, that just happened."

The door looming across the elevator was still there when Klawisz came back to threaten it with the crowbar. Not that Klawisz had expected it to move, but all the same, some part of him deep in his gut had sort of hoped it might have disappeared. He tapped the end of the crowbar against the side of his boot and sized the door up. Turning to make sure the elevator hadn't magically appeared behind him with disapproving Dashiell in tow, Klawisz pulled the crowbar up to chest height.

The elevator shaft remained quiet, the and the cables did't move. *All clear.*

He jammed the end of the crowbar into the side space between the door and the frame on the opposite side of its hinge in line with the door handle. He fiddled with the placement until he was sure that the bar was between the latch plate and the strike. Klawisz pressed on the bar, until the latch compressed.

The wood splintered with the final push that broke the door open. Klawisz stumbled as the crowbar came free, and caught himself on the window. He laughed in success, and grabbed the still locked handle to pull the door toward him. Klawisz rested the crowbar on his shoulder as he stared into the doorway.

He checked the windows again.

Nothing but air was on the other side of the wall from where the door was situated. The outside world still mocked him, with people coming and going, but he only had eyes for the outside wall of the hotel. Klawisz checked the windows on both sides. Twice. No matter how many times he looked, there was only brick on the other side of that doorway. His grip on the crowbar tightening with every second that he couldn't account for what he was seeing. Even for a place with dancing ghosts in the basements, giant insects, and staff that appeared and disappeared at will, this complete disregard for physics was a little on the odd side. Klawisz rubbed his mouth, and stood in the center of the open doorway.

The door didn't open up to the outside of the building like Klawisz had originally predicted, hoping to find a way to climb the outside of the building and forgoing the blasted locked doors, but instead this new passageway opened up into another hallway.

A very long hallway with bright, working lights on the walls, clean carpets, and a single door at the far end.

Klawisz reached out with the end of the crowbar and tapped it on the carpet just past the threshold. The iron bar made contact, smacking lightly onto the plush carpet on the floating hallway. Still not trusting the stability of the new pathway, Klawisz searched the area for something else to test it with. A pebble he found in a plant pot served his purpose. Klawisz tossed the pebble down the hallway and it bounced halfway down.

Klawisz threw the plant pot next.

It shattered about a third of the way down, but the hallway seemed to maintain its structure. It didn't flicker, didn't disappear. Still seemed solid.

Klawisz gripped tightly to the crowbar, squeezing hard. What sort of corridor like that only had one door?

He didn't trust it.

Klawisz marked the door on his map, made an extra note for it in his leather journal on a second thought, and went back to exploring the other doors on the fourth floor. The crowbar made his kicking method obsolete, and he was able to pry open the doors that didn't match his key in record time. The heels of his boots thanked him for the break to the increased wear and tear they had been experiencing.

When he found nothing as interesting as the floating hallway, the booze room, or the drunk corpse in any of the other rooms, Klawisz went back to the open stairwell door and headed up.

Maybe the fifth floor would have better luck.

CHAPTER 8

THERE WAS NOTHING on the fifth floor.

Almost literally. Klawisz whistled as he pried open the fifth floor stairwell door and was greeted by the open space. He grabbed the map from the wall out of habit, and snorted at the layout of rooms and doors that had once been on this floor. The map was a bit out of date, and rather useless at the moment, as most of the fifth floor had been torn down.

Walls, doors, floorboards, all of it had been stripped to the concrete slab. All that remained were plumbing pipes and electrical conduit that cut through the floor and disappeared into the ceiling, continuing the stacked utility layout of the building. He spotted ductwork doing the same, but for some reason the exposed utilities made the floor seem even more barren than if it had been completely vacant.

Klawisz leaned on the stairwell door frame, fighting a yawn. Smacking his cheeks to wake himself up, he took a step onto the stained concrete. Crossing the open area, he tapped the crowbar on his shoulder as he looked around the floor. Klawisz tread around the looming pipes as he went to the edge of the building, glancing at the chalk marks on the floor that marked where walls had once been. The room windows lined the far wall, all of them evenly spaced and unaware that the guest rooms that had once blocked them out were gone. He took a glance down one, and watched the people in the parking lot scurry by in the midday sun.

He tapped the crowbar against the bottom of the floorboard and kept walking, lifting his foot up and over the loose debris scattered around his path. Klawisz tapped the tip of his boot on the ground, twisting it on the dusty concrete. If there was anything useful on this floor, he wasn't seeing

46

it. To the left, though, something caught his eye.

Klawisz trotted to the area where the center seating area would have been, taking only a moment to mourn the lack of vending machines, before looking down through the open elevator pit. The iron safety gates were gone, leaving only a large square carved out of the concrete below and above him where the hole for the car should be. He stayed a good full two feet away from the hole, leaning over only as far as he'd dare to look down into the shaft. He had expected to see a service ladder of some sort in the corners, but as far as he could tell there wasn't any way to get up or down the shaft that wasn't the elevator car.

The pit was quiet, though it made its presence known with a soft wind that blew through the open space and ruffled the front of Klawisz's hair. The cords that held the elevator car remained still; the car not moving. He backed away and shivered, rubbing his arms through his sleeves and clutching his precious crowbar.

Nothing was going to get him back in that damn elevator.

Nothing.

Klawisz kept on past the hole in the ground and headed to the other side of the hotel. It was there, that he spotted something interesting: A door.

There was a door, standing up right where approximately the fourth room from the stairwell would be. He checked the metal numbers, and confirmed it when he read "05-08" hanging on the front of the door just below the peep hole. Klawisz walked a circle around the door, amused at this single thing standing tall on an otherwise destroyed floor.

For kicks, he grabbed the handle and twisted the knob.

It was locked.

His key didn't work either, and that gave him a moment of relief. Klawisz wasn't sure he wanted his room to be on the fifth floor if this was the state of things. Wondering if he'd find another mystery door like on the fourth floor, he decided to go ahead and crack it open with the crowbar. Klawisz almost laughed when open was all the door did.

No hidden hallway or secret room appeared out of nowhere, the door only swung out and left the empty frame with a hanging door in the hallway. Klawisz stepped through it for kicks, and tapped the crowbar on the frame as he passed. He shut the door behind him, smiling wistfully as the door's automatic lock clicked back into place.

As a gesture of good will, he reached up and locked the door chain from the other side.

Klawisz left the standing door be after his moment of fun, and headed to the stairwell on the opposite end of the building. He was about to jam his crowbar into the side to pry it open when he saw it: A steel cover over the space between the handle and the doorframe. Klawisz checked the door hinge: Also reinforced.

No amount of prying, kicking or screaming could get that second stairwell door open.

Something settled in Klawisz' stomach like a rock. He clutched to his precious crowbar, the one beacon of hope he had found in this place and turned tail to run to the other stairwell.

The stairwell doorway to the sixth floor on the other side was as reinforced and barred as the fifth floor one. After going through the trouble to get it, his crowbar was rendered useless in his progression through the hotel. He clung to it all the same.

Klawisz was trapped.

He sat in the stairwell with his back to the sixth floor door, legs spread out. The brandy bottle he'd found was in one hand and Klawisz had taken a tiny, much needed sip. He held the crowbar tight to his chest with his other hand, almost cuddling it like a security blanket. Klawisz was running out of options.

His pen markings on the fire escape maps stared up at him as he unfolded the mass of them from his pockets. Klawisz flipped through them one at a time, looking at the checked off rooms. He knew for certain that his room wasn't on the first, third, or fourth floor. It was possible that it could be on the second, but even with a crowbar and a pistol, Klawisz wasn't sure he was prepared to tangle with the local, eight legged resident there.

If his room was on the fifth floor, than there was nothing there to find. Klawisz took another sip from his bottle. His room couldn't be there. The scratched out number on his key had to refer to something other than "Your room has been leveled." Which meant he needed to keep looking on the other floors of the building, but they were blocked!

The elevator was not an option.

Klawisz folded up his maps and shoved them in his pockets. He'd go back down to the third or first floor and check the sixth stairwell doorway from the other side. Maybe the extra door security wasn't implemented on that side. Consistency didn't seem to be a factor in the hotel, so perhaps that was the luck still on his side. He could still get higher.

This line of thinking proved to be false.

The lower floor stairwell doors that he had yet to break into all had the extra steel plate covering the latch and strike plate. And all of them were just as impenetrable as the door blocking his way on the sixth floor. Klawisz ran a hand through his hair and squeezed the crowbar.

Those weren't there before.

They couldn't have been there before.

He turned around and headed back to the third floor to search the rooms he'd opened again. There had to be something he was missing. A key sitting around. A better way to go through or into a door, like an ax or a screwdriver. There had to be some way to keep searching rooms that didn't involve the elevator or going into the floating hallway.

A few hours later, and Klawisz had exhausted his options. He'd double checked every room he could open. He found rooms that he couldn't break down with his boot earlier newly equipped with crowbar proof steel plates and the thought they had materialized from the air when he hadn't been looking churned his stomach. His palms sweat. Klawisz stomped through the halls, ignoring the elevator cables as they began to move, echoing in the hallway and reminding him of the blasted thing's existence.

He would not use the elevator!

Klawisz stood in the middle of the empty fifth floor. Breathing heavily from his panicked running around the other floors. He clutched his crowbar, and leaned against a pipe. Even the vending machines he had broken into earlier were now fixed, and the glass reinforced with metal wire guards. It was as if the building was fighting back against his vandalism.

And for all he knew, it was.

A hanging light bulb sparked on above his head, the cord waved back and forth lightly as a breeze drifted across the empty floor. Klawisz watched it warily from his resting place, and glared at it, daring it to go out again. His stomach growled, and his mouth followed by echoing it with a snarl of its own. He was hungry, tired, and the building itself was now conspiring against him.

"Why bother giving me the crowbar if you're going to do this!"

Klawisz shouted in the empty floor. His voice carried down the open space and he kicked the nearest plumbing stack. "I just want to go to my room!"

He swung his crowbar like a baseball bat into the nearest metal pipe. Klawisz listened to the clang, and felt the reverberations of it up his arm. It felt good. It felt so good. Klawisz hit the pipe again, and again until the sweat beaded down his brow and he was soaked and exhausted under his heavy peacoat.

Klawisz lifted the bar, ready for another strike when the world turned blurry. His empty stomach made itself known, pulling in on itself as he wobbled back. Klawisz clutched to the crowbar and stumbled a few steps. The room spun around him, and in a blink, Klawisz stared at the concrete floor. His cheek pressed against the rough surface, sending a shiver of cold down his body. Klawisz groaned as the ache in his head grew and his eyes struggled to stay open.

The world went black.

CHAPTER 9

"I TOOK THE trouble of making you a reservation at the family diner, Mr. Wiśniowski," the Concierge said, his sleazy face glaring down at Klawisz as he jerked awake in the lobby yet again. He pressed his back into the leather seat as the Concierge pinned him to the chair with his hands on the arm rests. The man huffed, "We take very good care of our guests here whether they want it or not. That includes you, Mr. Wiśniowski."

"I told you, I don't want any dinner reservations," Klawisz said, even as his traitorous stomach growled in time with his demand.

"Don't want, true, but need? Yes. You haven't eaten in days, and it's about time you filled that belly of yours. No one wants to keep track of you passing out all the time," the Concierge said. He pulled Klawisz out of the chair by the ear, the way a parent would scold an errant child. He yanked hard as he dragged Klawisz with an iron grip toward the side stairwell and a waiting attendant. "Mr. Bell will escort you to the family diner. They already have a table waiting, special just for you."

"I already said!" Klawisz argued, shoving the Concierge's hand off his ear. "That I didn't want it. I can't pay for it. I don't trust it. And I'll just —"

"Break another vending machine?" the Concierge snorted, taking hold of Klawisz's upper arm. His fingers felt like ice, and dug into his skin through the fabric of his coat and shirt. The Concierge continued with his nose in the air, setting Klawisz's teeth to grind. "Please, don't start up with that. We're onto you and your destructive tendencies, Mr. Wiśniowski, and that is no longer an option for you. Go. Eat. Young Bell here will make sure you get there."

Klawisz opened his mouth to argue further, but was cut off by the bellboy grabbing his arm in place of the Concierge. The kid smiled, all pearly white teeth and sparkling green eyes that looked like someone had stuck a couple of emeralds into the kid's skull. They were as unnatural as Dashiell's and he wondered for two seconds if they were related. All the same, the Concierge smirked at him and Klawisz hissed, "Let go."

"Come now, Mr. Wiśniowski," Bell said as if he were speaking to an elderly patient in a home. He took Klawisz's elbow, locking it with his own. Bell patted his arm gently, and nodded. "I'll be happy to escort you."

The boy had the strength of a lion, his hold on Klawisz's arm not budging for even a second. Between the bellboy, the Concierge and the Janitor, Klawisz was wondering what was in the food in this place to make them all such strongmen. It couldn't be healthy, whatever it was. Bell pulled a keyring off his belt and opened the newly repaired and locked stairwell doorway. He dragged Klawisz with him to the other side, stopping only for a moment as Bell took care to lock the door again after himself. The temptation to steal the keyring from the kid burned at Klawisz's fingertips.

Only the kid's youth and Klawisz's guilt at the thought of knocking out a teenager stopped him.

Bell's brunette hair bounced under his cap as he turned to say, "I do wish you'd reconsider taking the elevator. It's a much faster way to get where you want to go."

"You might be able to drag me into one of those restaurants, but no force on earth is getting me back in that elevator," Klawisz said. Bell watched him with an eyebrow raised, and narrowed eyes. Something flashed behind them, almost suspicious. Judging. Klawisz steeled himself and held his ground. "I don't trust that thing, and I am never using it again."

"I wouldn't say things like that for certain," Bell said. He hummed as they walked down the stairs, linked arms and all. He leaned on Klawisz, squeezing his arm. "Things change a lot around here, minds included."

Klawisz's arm felt warm where Bell touched him. He wished it were comforting, but instead it sweltered. "We'll see about that."

"I will," Bell said, dropping his head on Klawisz's shoulder. He held a finger up and spun it in the air with an amused laugh. "Just as I'm sure you'll enjoy your dinner. They really do have the best food here, and Julie makes the best drinks."

Bell straightened and pulled on Klawisz's arm with an air of urgency a second later. "But don't tell Annie I said that!"

"I won't," Klawisz said, shaking his head. "Secret's safe with me."

"Good to hear," Bell finished. "I'd hate for either of those sisters to be cross with me. But that's another matter! I'm sure you want to get to dinner instead of listening to me gossip."

Klawisz grunted, and his free hand gripped the air, already missing his crowbar. He hoped it was still on the fifth floor where he'd fallen, or he was going to have a word with that Concierge.

"Let's just get this over with," Klawisz muttered, shoving his hands in his pockets as they stepped down the next few rungs of stairs.

"That's the spirit!" Bell said, his laugh ringing like his namesake.

The door was locked when they arrived, but no sooner had Bell knocked on the front of the glass, Klawisz could hear the bolts being undone with loud clacks, and the switch of a lock being opened quickly followed.

A perky face greeted them: a young woman in her twenties had opened the door, wearing a uniform that matched Annie's in the bar next door. Her lipstick was pink, a subtle shade when put up against the dark blue eye shadow and heavily blushed red cheeks.

"Thanks for bringing him here, Bell," she said. The bellboy discretely released Klawisz's arm when he noticed that his victim wasn't going to make a run for it. Amused, the girl pointed at Klawisz with her index finger, thumb raised like she was firing a gun, and winked. "Been waiting for you since Annie said you stopped by the bar."

"You must be Julie," Klawisz said, remembering the name alongside the sweet taste of fizzing juice. "She said you make a great cocktail."

"I do, but none for you. The only thing you're getting is a filling meal," Julie said. She waved her finger at him, indicating that Klawisz should follow. "I'll take it from here, kiddo."

"Yes, ma'am," Bell said. He gave a small goodbye way to Klawisz and skipped down the hallway.

In a blink he was gone, long before he reached the door.

"Now then," Julie said. She held the door open, and motioned again for Klawisz to follow. "Let's get some food into your belly, hm?"

The room just beyond the door smelled of burnt dust, like someone had turned on a floorboard heater for the first time in an old house. He scrunched his nose and followed her inside, stepping over a sizable cockroach that scurried across the room. Klawisz jumped as the door slammed behind him. Julie mechanically locked the door with the key that was on her belt, and bolted the top. She grinned at him, and said a quick, "Follow me."

Klawisz trailed behind her through a small diner full of dust covered tables, caked so thick Klawisz could swear there was a full inch of it. The cockroaches in the corners were the least of his worries when he saw the cobwebs hung from the overhead lights, connecting them together with the weavings of the spiders. Klawisz kept his hands in his pockets. Julie kept walking, taking him past an old buffet line with stained glass sneeze guards. The trays were empty of food, but held quite the collection of insects and moths.

"Don't let the decor bother you," Julie said. She hummed lightly and came to a door in the back with thick glass panels in the wood. They showed pictures of suns and moons. Stars and the universe. Klawisz shivered, and wrapped his arms around himself thinking of Dashiell and his eyes. Julie ignored his discomfort, and pulled her key ring back up. She unlocked the door, and opened it. "Because you'll be dining in our private VIP room here. The Concierge said you could use it, lucky you!"

The private dining room was clean and bright, reminding Klawisz of the lobby transforming from dirt and dust to gold and glitter. Every surface was freshly painted, and the flatware on the tables shined as they sat on top of the bright table cloths. Six tables were scattered throughout the small room, three of which were booths alongside the wall. Julie led him to the center booth, and helped Klawisz to a seat.

Julie pulled a small notebook from the front of her apron, and pulled a pencil down from behind her ear. She winked and asked, "What can I get you?"

Klawisz shifted, awkward and alone in the small room. He looked around the table for a menu, and shrugged when he failed to find one. "What do you have?"

"Name it and I'll get it," Julie said. She tapped the front of the pad with her pencil tip, up and down in a practiced, natural manner. "We treat our guests well here, Mr. Wiśniowski. Whatever you want, is our treat."

He closed his eyes and inhaled, thinking of his home away from home.

Of his grandmother's cooking, her cosy kitchen, and the vase full of poppies that was always in the center of his table. He remembered sitting at her table at dinner, and he could almost smell his favorite meal as if it were in the room now. Leaving his daydream, Klawisz dawned a wry smile as he asked, "Any chance I could get *gołąbki*?"

"With parsley mashed potatoes," Julie said, writing down the order. She tapped her pencil up and down on the writing pad, shifting her weight onto one leg and cocking her hip to the side. "You've got it, honey. Can I get you a drink to go with that?"

Klawisz' jaw fell as the request was accepted without hesitation. She even knew what side dishes his grandmother made with it. In his slightly stunned state, he managed to ask for coffee and a glass of water.

Might help him wake up.

"It'll be up in just a bit," Julie said. She stuffed the notebook and pencil back into her apron, and placed a basket of bread rolls on the table with a small plate. "You just sit there and relax and I'll be right back before you know it."

Julie left Klawisz alone, disappearing as he turned to look at the table. He slumped in his seat and rested his head on the back seat of the booth. After updating his entry on the staff in his journal, Bell included, he closed his eyes and pretended not to see the monarch butterfly that landed on the table in the middle of the room.

The *gołąbki* were perfect.

The tiny pigeon shaped rolls of boiled cabbage wrapped around the succulent pork were heaven on a plate. He could smell the onions and barley coming from the inside of the leafy wrap, and it nearly brought Klawisz to tears when he cut into the roll and ate a bite of the juicy, moist food, savoring the lingering taste of the tomato cream sauce.

It was the best thing he'd ever eaten.

He made sure to tell Julie as such as he tore into the mashed potatoes. He wiped the side of his mouth with a napkin after he drank down a gulp of water to make room for more. He felt a bit like Bell when he tacked on a quick, "But don't tell the Concierge I said that."

Julie chuckled lightly with one hand on her hip and the other holding a pot of coffee. She leaned over Klawisz as he ate like a wild animal, days of hunger catching up to the sheer joy of having good *gołąbki* in his stomach again. When his plate was cleared, she poured a cup of coffee.

"Thought you might want this after the meal rather than during," Julie said. She pulled the cup the side and added cream and sugar, swirling it once with a spoon. Julie switched his empty plate for the cup of coffee, twisting the cup just so. "Let me know if you'd like anything else, but you're free to go now that we don't have to worry about you passing out. Just make sure you lock the door after you when you leave, honey.

"Oh! And this time let the Concierge know if you get hungry again, too," Julie said. She waved with her fingers and unlocked the small room's door with the key on her belt. "I hope you enjoy the rest of your stay, Mr. Wiśniowski."

Klawisz half listened, head bowed over the coffee cup as he heard her lock the door after her. He inhaled the steam from the cup, unaware and aware at the same time when he came to be alone in the room. Just Klawisz, the cup of coffee, and the odd symbol clear as day written in a swirl of cream on the top layer of the dark liquid.

It was like some eldritch marking, that was impossible to describe in any words or tongue that Klawisz knew. At the same time, the symbol burned itself into Klawsiz's memory. Locked there, much like every door in the building.

"I'm too tired for this," Klawisz said. He picked up the cup of coffee and tossed it back. When he put the cup back down, the symbol was gone and left the regular casual swirls of cream and sugar in the arabica coffee. "Way too tired."

He leaned back in the booth seat, sipping his coffee until he emptied the cup.

Klawisz pulled his room key from his pocket and held it in his palm on the table. All this time, and the poor little key had yet to find the door that would reveal what numbers had once been on the fob before they were scratched off. Klawisz's room. He closed his fingers around it and pushed away from the table. "Time to get back to work."

CHAPTER 10

SOMEONE HAD STOLEN his crowbar. Klawisz pouted, with one hand scratching the back of his head roughly as he stood on the empty floor where he had passed out. He dug his nails into his scalp, ruffling his hair and counting to ten before he screamed. Instead, he kicked a loose board from the ground and headed back to the stairs. There had to be someplace else he could go. The sixth floor stairwell was still blocked, and still impervious to his pre-crowbar room entering strategies.

Klawisz left the empty floor, scowling at the elevator shaft as he went. There *had* to be another way to the floors above.

What he needed was a key to those doors.

Keys.

"I think I need to pay the Janitor another visit," Klawisz said, clicking his tongue and heading back for the broken stairwell door. He skipped down the steps, flicking off the doorway to the second floor as he went and kept going down. "He'll have to help."

When he finally reached the utility floor, his legs burning from the sheer amount of stairs he'd descended, he found the Janitor had other plans.

"No," the old man hissed from behind the door on the lowest floor of the building. Klawisz knocked again on the door with his knuckles. The man shouted back with equal strength. "No! You can't have my keys!"

"Then how about an escort?" Klawisz tried, thinking it couldn't hurt. He licked his lips and asked through the door. "I just want to get to the upper floors."

"We have a perfectly good, working elevator," The Janitor shouted back, shuffling around on the other side of the wood. Klawisz could hear his keyring jingling as he moved, taunting him just beyond the door. "Use it!"

"I have a fear of elevators," Klawisz lied. He considered asking Bell to escort him around instead. The kid was much nicer and he had keys too, didn't he? But that meant he'd have to call the Concierge to get the lobby employees to appear, and Klawisz had no desire to talk to *him*. He'd have to convince the Janitor to help him out. Klawisz knocked on the door again. "And besides, the stairs are better for my health."

Klawisz heard the shift of a deadbolt, and the door swung open, revealing the fierce and angry Janitor. He hissed, "What's good for your health is for you to high tail your ass out of my basement and back upstairs."

"With the keys?" Klawisz asked.

"No," the door slammed shut and locked again. The next words out of the Janitor's mouth screamed "threat" in glowing letters. "You've got five minutes to get upstairs before I shove you back into that elevator again."

Klawisz pouted at the doorway and turned away. The Janitor didn't look so big. Maybe he could knock him out and steal the keys from him. Then again, nothing really was like it appeared around here was it? His previous memory of being manhandled like it was nothing had nothing to do with that second thought.

Honestly.

Klawisz backed away from the door, but in a quick decision of irrationality, he turned down another hallway to further explore the basement instead of heading up the stairs. He had five minutes.

Surely he could find something as good as a key?

Keeping a mental countdown of the time in his head before the Janitor came out of hiding to fetch him, Klawisz kicked down the first door he found out of earshot from the Janitor's closet. The door threw open, revealing an old storage room with packed shelves full of cleaners, tools and all sorts of other knick knacks that could be used in building maintenance. The overhead light didn't work, and Klawisz struggled to see in the dark.

"Could really use a flashlight," he mumbled under his breath, his mental clock still ticking down the seconds of his precious few minutes. Klawisz squinted at the shelves, pocketing anything that looked remotely helpful. He snatched a screwdriver, a book of matches, and some extra pens. "But I'll make do."

Klawisz shoved boxes aside, looking up and down the shelves. He ignored a stack of batteries and an old camera, continuing to look for anything he could use to open a door that had been bolted. Most of the storage room contained old junk, and he tipped over a box full of nuts and bolts. Nothing more useful than what he already had.

His countdown kept steady, his time nearly out with only one minute left. One minute to get to the stairs. Klawisz turned and backed out of the room when a shine of light from the hallway hit something just behind a shelf.

"Now that's the ticket," Klawisz whistled. He yanked the ax free from the space between the shelf and the wall. He held the heavy thing in his hand and grinned. "If I can't get a key, might as well have the next best thing."

Klawisz turned tail and ran for the stairs, laughing as he passed by the Janitor's door as it unlocked.

Klawisz dropped the head of the ax into the sixth floor stairwell door right on the mark next to the lock. He laughed, bringing the blade back down into the splintering wood and cheering as the entire doorknob clattered to the floor and the door bust open.

Into a world of fire.

Klawisz scrambled away from the open door, covering his mouth with his hand as the flames burst forth from the hallway, smoke climbing up and hitting the ceiling as his back hit the side wall. The entire sixth floor burned, everything aflame and coated in heat.

Fire licked the concrete ground of the landing as it spilled out from the doorway. Burning. Everything past the threshold and onto the sixth floor was mountains and rivers of fire. Hot, yellows and reds with quick licks of blue. Sweat beaded on Klawisz's forehead as the sheer heat of it escaped the floor and into the stairwell. His breath heaved and and clutched to the wooden handle of his ax.

"Room's not on that floor," Klawisz said to himself, licking his lips. "Definitely not that one."

He kept his back to the wall as he sidled around the corner toward the next flight up. By the time he made it to the middle landing between the sixth and seventh floors, he heard a slam as the door below was pulled shut by some outside force. Klawisz leaned over the railing to look, and saw smoke pour out from the gaps between the door and the frame. He swallowed and kept going up to the seventh floor.

Klawisz pulled himself up by the stairwell handle, a few steps at a time as he headed for the door above. He let the ax hang down by his side and checked the door. He tapped the door handle, and feeling it cool to the touch, grabbed it to make sure. Locked, but not hot. The chances of finding fire behind the door was minimal and had him raising the ax and slamming it down into the side of the handle. He chopped away until the handle fell off and he could shove the door open.

The seventh floor looked to be clear of fire, and that was enough. Klawisz stepped through the door, the ax up and ready for whatever may show in the guest rooms on this floor. After drunken corpses, giant scorpions and broken bottles, Klawisz was ready for just about anything.

He paused only to grab the map off the side door, tacking it on top of his stack.

Klawisz's key failed to work on the first six doors, but the ax worked well enough. Much like many of the other rooms in this hotel, Klawisz was greeted by clean empty rooms and dust. He scrunched his nose as he left them behind, and went to the seventh door. The ax opened it when his key would not, and Klawisz found himself throwing his arms up to protect his face.

A wall of butterflies came pouring out of the room door. Thousands upon thousands of them in all colors and shapes and sizes, from ones as small as his little finger to as large as his torso. Reds, greens, sparkling and dull. Butterflies everywhere in a massive wall of wings.

Klawisz fell on his backside as they fluttered above his head, reflecting the dim light of the lights on the walls. A shining, glorious sight that had his back against the floor.

They flew above his head, a beautiful mass of colorful insects for a few moments longer before they scattered. The flapping of their wings was a roar of sound, echoing over Klawsiz's head as he stared up into the mass of them from the ground. The wind they created tugged and pulled on his hair as the butterflies rushed to the end of the hallway like an undertow. They disappeared out the open fire door, they flew away as quickly as they arrived.

Klawisz used his ax as a crutch as he pushed himself into a sitting position. He stared into the Butterfly Room, listening to the soft sound of something breathing beyond the dark threshold. Klawisz dragged himself up the wall until he was standing, and peeked his head through the door. He held his breath.

A giant butterfly rested in the middle of the room.

Massive in size, it bent the mattress of the bed, its thick and heavy body weighing it down. Klawisz's grip on his ax loosened as his shoulders dropped and he took in the sight. The butterfly's wingspan filled the entire room, the tips of the wings touching the ceiling as they flicked. Soft dust fluttered off the wings, filling the space with a fog that lingered in the air. The wings were near iridescent, the colors mesmerizing. With each flap, a ripple descended across the scale-like wings changing the colors in a wave. From blue to pink to green to yellow and so forth. An endless stream of colors.

Klawisz backed away and gently shut the door, his heart pounding in his chest so hard he thought he might pass out again.

Next room.

After failing to capture the true beauty and terror of the butterfly in his journal with his mediocre sketches, Klawisz continued his search of the seventh floor. Methodically checking the doors as he had done when he first started looking on the first floor, he reminded himself that his search was over halfway finished. One by one he found them locked, a mismatch for his room key, and then busted them down with the ax.

The monotony of the exercise created a weariness that Klawisz felt deep in his soul. Was it so horrible that he wanted to find his room? It seemed that was true as he checked the last room on the floor. With a heavy sigh, Klawisz broke the stairwell door down and stepped onto the stairwell landing. He pulled himself up the steps, one foot after the other at a time.

The eighth floor door came open with a clatter, and he grabbed the map.

He checked ten rooms before a little excitement made itself known.

Door eleven opened to reveal a rather large Flying Ant, as mutated and deformed as his distant cousin hanging out on the second floor. Pock marks and raised bumps covered every surface, mixed in with elongated hairs coming off its limbs. Giant glimmering wings hung off the Ant's back, smacking together loudly as they flickered.

Already missing the monotony of before, Klawisz made a run for it as giant pincers made a grab for his leg. He feet pounded down the hallway when he remembered the gun. The weight of it in his peacoat pocket slapped against his thigh as he moved. The Ant was slower than the Scorpion, but more agile. If he got down the hall fast enough to get some distance between them, there was no way he couldn't shoot it.

When Ant got distracted by one of the flickering lights on the wall, Klawisz ripped open his pocket and pulled out—a piece of paper wrapped around a paperweight? He ripped the paper off the gun-shaped iron block and read a note written in calligraphy:

It's not nice to steal, Mr. Wiśniowski. Tsk, tsk.
-The Concierge

"What!" Klawisz shouted, his hand crumbling around the note. Rage filled his veins, and somehow the Ant was forgotten as he imagined beating the Concierge head in with the iron block in his hand. Klawisz went for enraged yelling, but it sounded more like a whine when he cried out: "I didn't even get to use it yet!"

His yell grabbed the attention of the Ant, and it rose off the ground with the slick wings on its back. He pretended the Ant's head was the Concierge's face and threw the paperweight at it as hard as he could. He missed, and the Ant flew fast toward Klawisz like a barreling steam train down a track. Blood rushing, he did the only thing he could. His brain acting on its own, and before he could blink, Klawisz lifted the ax above his head and he swung it down hard as the Ant approached.

It hit dead center in the Ant's head, smacking it to the ground, pincers and all. With adrenaline pumping in his veins and the only thing moving his limbs, Klawisz ripped the ax out from between the Ant's antennae and brought it down again. The head of the ax smacked into the side of the Ant's torso. A third hit tore off a wing with a heavy crunch.

Like a mad man, he brought the ax up and down repeatedly until the ant stilled. Klawisz's chest heaved as he stood above the beast, the head of the ax buried in the exoskeleton of the now dead Flying Ant. He swallowed, and rubbed on the back of his neck with a sigh. Maybe he didn't need the gun after all. Klawisz had this handled with just the ax!

As he caught his breath, he heard a sizzling sound. A hiss combined with a bubble that sounded like a pop. Klawisz yanked the ax out of the Ant's head and grimaced seeing the hot sludge that covered the ax head spilling out of the Ant. He held it away from himself as the sizzling grew louder and ate away at the metal. Plops of the odd substance hit the ground, continuing to cook anything it touched. The slop ate straight through the carpet, and as it climbed up its way from the handle, Klawisz dropped the tool.

His ax was devoured in a heartbeat, leaving Klawisz with no ax, no crowbar and no gun.

CHAPTER 11

WITHOUT HIS TOOLS, there was only one door open that Klawisz could turn to: The floating hallway on the fourth floor.

He stood in front of the open door, staring at the shattered pot that he'd thrown earlier. Klawisz licked his lips, and held a foot ready to cross the threshold. The world outside had already turned to night, hiding anything past the windows in darkness. He couldn't have double checked the lack of hallway outside even if he wanted to. Klawisz scrunched his eyes shut, grit his teeth and took the step.

The hallway held his weight.

Klawisz took another step, and another. The ground remained solid enough after a few feet, no hint of the ground falling out from under him as his boots strode on the carpet. After a few more paces, Klawisz opened his eyes. The door behind him slammed shut, and Klawisz turned around with a spin. He dashed back for the door he'd come through, and tugged on the handle, rattling it.

It wouldn't budge.

His chest heaved as his pulse increased. Klawisz banged on the door a few more times for good measure when the light on the wall to his left flickered out. The one to his right soon followed. Klawisz turned away from the door, and watched as the lights on the walls blinked off, one by one heading down the corridor. As the remaining lit lights got further and further away, Klawisz's corner got darker and darker.

With no source of light, he'd be alone in the dark in a matter of seconds.

Klawisz sprinted for the other end of the hallway, chasing after the lit lights. There was a door at the other end. He couldn't break down the door he'd come in from, but surely the other one! Klawisz easily caught up with the lights as they blinked out, and ran faster to pass them.

A rush of cold air filled the hallway, ruffling Klawisz's hair. Something loomed in the dark at the end of the hallway he'd come from. Heavy thumps shook the ground, growing louder and louder by the second. Something was coming, following the lights as they turned off one by one. Letting the darkness catch up with him was not an option. The shadows chased him, nipping at his ankles.

Klawisz sprinted faster, his chest and legs burning like the sixth floor.

He crashed into the door at the end, his fingers searching desperately for the handle. Klawisz looked behind as the lights continued to blink out behind him and the temperature continued to drop. His teeth chattered together and he whined, "Come on, come on!"

The door was locked, but instead of a key hole there was a slide puzzle built into the door.

Klawisz felt the walls closing in on him. Perhaps they weren't really moving or they were, all he truly knew was the looming darkness was getting closer and closer and sound of thudding footfalls was getting louder and louder and the lock on this door was a slide puzzle.

He hissed, and banged his fist on the upper door and breathed out. His breath was a fog of white, and his fingers were turning blue. Klawisz counted to ten. Had to concentrate. Focus. *Focus.*

Complete the puzzle, escape the dark. Simple enough. Klawisz rubbed his cheek before looking at the pieces. He had eighteen to move into place and no idea what picture he was making. He shifted the pieces around as the sound of each light popping out behind him grew louder by the second. They sounded like gunshots going off, one by one, threatening to burst his eardrums with the noise.

Bang.

"Going to hit the Concierge for taking my gun," Klawisz growled to himself as he shifted pieces. He lined two up and blinked at the swirl it formed. He'd seen that before. Klawisz shifted the pieces faster, grinning like a loon. "The symbol in my coffee."

Bang.

He recreated the symbol he'd seen in the cream and dark liquid he'd had at the diner, finishing the puzzle as the last few lights blinked out behind him. His fingers trembled as he jammed the last piece into place, his heart screaming in his chest with the weight of its pounding.

Completed, the puzzle glowed brightly, backlit from behind the pieces. It hissed before a loud clack could be heard on the other side of the door.

Bang.

He'd unlocked it.

Klawisz slammed into the door, tumbling through and falling flat on his face on the other side. He groaned, rubbing his cheek into cheap carpet, listening as the door slammed shut behind him.

"You do get around, don't you, Mr. Wiśniowski?" Dashiell said, sitting on an old couch against the wall.

Klawisz stayed face down on the carpet.

Maybe if he didn't move he'd wake up in his bed in his room and the elevator operator wouldn't be laughing at him with his crooked nose and perfect teeth. Klawisz groaned and rubbed at his eyes before rolling onto his back. Dashiell's odd, star field eyes twinkled so obnoxiously in amusement Klawisz considered punching the man and breaking his nose all over again. Instead, he took the offered hand and let Dashiell pull him to his feet.

Across the room, Annie and Bell played a game of cards on a folding table. They mostly ignored Dashiell and Klawisz in favor of their game, though he caught a few amused glances in their direction.

Klawisz tugged on his hand in an attempt to retrieve it, however, Dashiell held onto it. His grip was secure and warm, and had no intention of letting go. Klawisz let him keep holding his hand for the moment without a fuss and asked, "Where am I?"

"The break room," Dashiell said. He tugged Klawisz away from the door, shaking his head. "We don't allow guests back here, you know."

"Well, this definitely wasn't where I was trying to go," Klawisz said. Dashiell squeezed his hand and dragged Klawisz away from the door he'd crashed through and to a door on a perpendicular wall. "If that helps."

"Where were you trying to go?" Dashiell asked, his tone full of laughter. Thankfully, the tone was fond and kind instead of mocking. He knocked his knuckles on the second break room door three times, paused, and two more knocks. "Still looking for your room?"

"Something like that," Klawisz said. Dashiell opened the door and Klawisz got a good look at a garden. Fresh flowers and plants grew everywhere, and the smell of honey wafted through the doorway. Dashiell closed the door with a frown and tapped his knuckles on the door four times, waited and then another two. "If the Concierge told me where my room was, I'd be more than happy to stop bothering everyone."

"Believe me, if he could, he would," Dashiell said, sighing heavily. He opened the door again and cheered. "Ah! There we go: the lobby."

"The lobby?" Klawisz asked.

Dashiell let go of his hand and pressed Klawisz on the lower back through the door. "The lobby."

Klawisz fell through the exit, and his feet tripped out into the dust covered lobby floor. He turned around to see Dashiell wave before solidly closing the door. Klawisz looked up and saw the "Employees Only" sign above his head and backed away from the door.

The lobby remained empty, trapped in dust. The Concierge's bell sat proudly in place on his desk, but Klawisz walked right by it. He wasn't asking for help from that bastard.

He intended to make his way straight to the stairwell to maybe try the basement again when a flash of something caught his eye. Klawisz turned and saw a small lump sitting on the edge of the check-in desk. Upon closer inspection, Klawisz discovered the lump to be something rather impressive:

A flashlight.

He picked the small item up and turned the black plastic over in his hand. It was a good size, and the head at the top was on a swivel so that he could move the light back and forth from a straight light to an L-Shaped light. Klawisz clicked the light on and it shined brightly in the dilapidated lobby.

"There's no way this was here the entire time," Klawisz said to himself, clicking the light on and off a few times. "Not a chance I just walked by it."

On the counter he saw the outline of where the flashlight had been in the dust. He brushed dust off the side of the flashlight, and shoved it in his front coat upper pocket.

Klawisz blew a strand of hair out of his face and rolled his eyes. "Or maybe that's exactly what I did."

At least now he had a light.

CHAPTER 12

THIRTEEN FLOORS ABOVE ground level, and four sub levels.

Klawisz had explored most of the sub levels, and seven of the thirteen upper floors. Still no sign of his room.

The eighth floor stairwell door mocked Klawisz.

No crowbar, no ax, and the door was impervious to the kick of his heel. The door handle was also, of course, locked. Klawisz needed something to open this door. Something big. Klawisz backed up until he hit the back wall of the stairwell. He crossed his arms and sucked in a breath. He needed something powerful. Turning his head to the side, he saw a case on the wall next to the fire extinguisher hidden in the dark where the light just didn't reach.

Klawisz flicked on the flashlight in his pocket.

A shotgun would work just fine.

Klawisz used the butt of the flashlight to break the glass of the security case. It shattered around his feet and Klawisz pulled down the weapon from the wall. He found a package of slugs in the bottom of the case and snorted. He had no idea why there was a shotgun hanging in a glass case on the wall of a hotel stairwell, but he wasn't going to question it.

It was the least the hotel could do after taking his revolver before he had a chance to fire it.

He pulled the bolt out and loaded two slugs into the chamber. Klawisz slammed the bolt back into place and walked up to the door.

"This is so stupid," Klawisz laughed as he lined up the barrel sight with the door knob. He aimed just for the left of the knob, careful to point down so that the bullet would pass through the door and into the concrete. Klawisz turned off the safety and put his finger on the trigger.

"So damn stupid."

He pulled the trigger anyway.

The deafening blast of the shotgun covered the sound of the wood cracking open as the slug burst through the door, shattering the lock and leaving a hole about the size of his fist. The loose bits of wood and dust floated to the ground.

Klawisz giggled as his body trembled from the power of the weapon. His shoulder ached from where the ricochet of the gun slammed it into his flesh past the peacoat, but it was a good hurt. Klawisz yanked the remainder of the toppled door handle out of the door and shoved it open.

The lights on the eight floor had gone out, and he looked down to see the leftovers of the shotgun slug buried into the concrete floor, a burn in the carpet. Klawisz slung the gun under his arm and reached up for the eighth floor map.

He dug out his key and his pen and set to work checking the rooms.

Things were finally starting to look up around here.

In higher spirits, Klawisz managed to check the eighth, ninth, and tenth floors in record time.

He didn't find the room that matched his key, but for his troubles, Klawisz collected four more boxes of shotgun ammunition, a package of batteries for his newly acquired flashlight, a video camera with odd footage on it from some sort of medical facility, a new appreciation for the depth of his coat pockets and for the durability of his room key.

It was getting plenty of practice on all these doors that didn't fit its grooves.

Klawisz stopped in front of the eleventh floor entrance, and gave the door one chance to stay in tact by attempting to kick it open. Happy that it turned down this opportunity, he loaded the gun and blew off the door handle with the practiced ease he'd gained from three floors of aiming.

He flicked on his flashlight as he walked into the darkened hall.

The lights flickered on and off randomly one at a time, flashing the hallway in a tiny burst of lights in random places, reminding him of the second floor. Klawisz held tight to the shotgun and aimed the flashlight ahead of him as he stepped into the hallway. He tugged the fire map free from its plastic case and tried the first door.

And then the next and the next.

By the time he reached the middle foyer with the elevator, his stomach growled and he'd worked up a sweat in the dark. A heat lingered on this floor, oppressive and heavy.

Klawisz broke the glass of the vending machine with the back end of the shotgun (he loved this gun so much he wanted to carve his name into the base) and pulled out a few snacks. The elevator cable rumbled behind him as he ripped into a package of old chocolate candies. He munched on a handful as he listened to the rusty gate behind him screech open. A light from the elevator car flooded the dark lobby, casting his shadow on the broken vending machine.

Dashiell poked his head out of the elevator car and hummed. "You wouldn't be interested in a lift, would you?"

"Nope," Klawisz said, patting the barrel of his shotgun. "Got it covered from here."

"I can see that," Dashiell said, his sparkling eyes and mouth smiling together as one. He leaned on the edge of the elevator car's open gate and crossed his arms over his chest. "And hear. You're making quite the racket up here. I think you've aged the Concierge about a hundred years since you started walking around."

"Well, if he told me where my room was when I first asked, we wouldn't be having this problem," Klawisz said. He pulled his key up and jangled it in front of the light of his flashlight. "As I've brought up before."

"Well, everyone has to find their own room, their own way, I suppose," Dashiell said. He took a step back into the car and wrapped his fingers around the control. "Are you sure I can't offer you a lift? This elevator goes all the the way to the top."

"I've only got two floors left, Dash," Klawisz said. He crumbled his empty chocolate wrapper and threw it in the garbage can to the left of the potted plant. Klawisz shrugged his shoulders and saluted Dashiell from the side of his head. "Who'd give up all this stubbornness with only two to go?"

Dashiell laughed, hearty and joyful, and slammed the gate closed. He scrunched his nose and his eyes continued their universe glimmer as he pulled the control handle to the car. Dashiell bowed his head as the car jerked and began to move. "Touché, Mr. Wiśniowski."

The elevator car rattled as it descended down the floors.

Klawisz checked the scribbles on his map, and continued to explore the rest of the eleventh floor.

Two to go.

He slipped his key into the next door on the list and rattled it. No match, but he had to be coming up on his door soon. Had to.

If it wasn't on the twelfth or thirteenth floor, Klawisz wasn't sure what he'd do.

The fifth floor was gone, the sixth was on fire and he'd checked the rest. Klawisz shook his head and kicked his heel into the door. There was no place for those thoughts in his mind, not after he'd come so far.

As he cleared the eleventh floor with no success, he sucked in a breath.

Two to go.

CHAPTER 13

KLAWISZ KICKED THE twelfth floor door open with the side of his boot, shoving aside the shattered pieces of the doorknob and broken wood.

The shotgun was hot in his hands and the floor pitch black. The light from his flashlight disappeared into the void of it, giving him a few inches of light as he stepped fully onto the floor. Klawisz kept the gun up, and eyes searching. The darkness loomed before him like a monster under the bed; never sure if it was there or not. Waiting. Klawisz reloaded the weapon, making sure it had both shots ready. Klawisz reached for the floor map, wincing when his hand came back with a cut.

He sucked on the tiny wound, and flashed his light up on the wall.

The glass case that held the map was shattered, the fire safety map crumbled away and torn. Klawisz sucked on the edge of his finger one more time before putting both hands on the gun. He had four rounds left, including the two already loaded. If something was going to come at him, he'd better make those shots count.

Klawisz inched forward in the dark, his flashlight illuminating the particles floating in the air. Someone or something had disturbed the dust on this floor.

"Now where are you?" Klawisz whispered. His shoes clung to the carpet as he moved, like walking through dried and sticky soda. It smelled sugary and old, feeling unclean in a whole new way. Klawisz heard his own heartbeat in the hallway, echoing like it'd been connected to a loudspeaker. "In a room, or in a hallway?"

He stopped and checked the nearest door to him. The hanging letters read "12-03" in their embossed plaques.

"Okay, get your act together," Klawisz told himself. He scowled at the door before straightening his back. "You're only two rooms down the hallway."

He'd never find his room at this rate.

Darkness or not, *monsters or not*, Klawisz was going to find his room.

And he was going to take a nap. A long, deep nap on clean bedding with a fluffy pillow under his head. He had plans to become one with the mattress, sleeping sound enough not even the Concierge could wake him up.

"Let's go back and do this right," Klawisz said. He stuck his key into the first door in the hallway, and twisted. Locked. Instead of breaking down the door, Klawisz moved onto the next door. "I can come back for supplies. Right now I just want this to be done."

One half of the hallway cleared, and the darkness was no longer the only thing pressing down on Klawisz's soul. He had one more floor and half a hallway to check. His options were running out, and the alternative wasn't something he wanted to think about.

As he passed the end of the first half of the hallway and stepped into the small lobby, Klawisz paused. The lights of the vending machines glowed, shining like ghosts in the corner. Empty of any treats or product, they served as useless beacons marking the hallway point of the corridor. Klawisz sighed at the empty machine, and huffed. He wasn't hungry yet, but this was a sign he'd have to visit the Concierge again to get food.

As if reading his mind, Klawisz heard the hum of the elevator cables moving behind him. A personal ferry down to the first floor arrived as if called. Klawisz snorted and tilted his head back as he heard a car stop. The rusted screech of the metal safety gates followed.

Klawisz dropped the shot gun to a loose hold under his arm, and ran a hand through the back of his hair. He turned toward the elevator, and said, "Look, Dashiell. I appreciate the concern, but I'm not taking the—"

He cut off, slamming his teeth together so fast he might have broken one.

A long, thin limb rested against the gate shoved against the wall. The rest of its body didn't sit inside an elevator car, but hung off the cables with its other arm and four legs covered in spines. A head dipped out of the open space, large bulbous eyes plastered on either side of its triangular head.

That wasn't Dashiell.

Klawisz booked it down the hallway toward the open stairwell door.

The Giant Mantis tore through the elevator door opening, its body taking up the entire width of the small hallway. Its forelegs were sharp as razors, and stronger than steel. He could hear them chipping the concrete floor through the carpeting and coverings with every heavy step.

The beast jerked in quick movements, each of its joints clicking and clacking. The quick flashes of his light made the monster appear and disappear in the darkness, its pose different with each glimpse. The Mantis swiped at the floor with its forelegs, tearing up the carpet and digging an inch into the concrete below.

Klawisz remembered a time in his grandmother's yard, when he had stumbled upon a mantis on a branch. It had caught a cricket by chance, and Klawisz watched in childish fascination as the mantis clutched to its food, eating it slowly bit by bit with the mandibles around its mouth. But the memory that stuck out the most, was that Klawisz remembered how the cricket had squirmed the entire time.

The mantis had eaten his prey alive.

That memory pushed Klawisz's legs to move faster than he had ever run in his life. Visions of getting caught and having his limbs eaten one at a time as he screamed and clawed to get away entered his head without permission. Klawisz had a feeling he wouldn't be so lucky as to lose his head first should the worst happen.

"Stop that!" Klawisz commanded of himself.

His shout caught the Mantis' attention, and he pushed himself faster. If he could get to the door, he could escape it the way he did the Scorpion on the second floor. There's no way it would fit through the door.

If there was a door.

Klawisz slammed into a solid wall when he reached the end of the hallway. His hand searched the wall where the doorknob should be, and met nothing but smooth plaster. He stepped back, letting the light shine over the entirety of the hallway door and sucked in a breath.

The door was gone.

It was gone.

Klawisz spun around fast, and pulled up the shotgun. He rested his back against the wall, his heart racing in his chest as he waited. The darkness that escaped his flashlight concealed the Mantis, leaving only the sounds of its thumping limbs as it took slow steps.

The hallway wasn't wide. The Mantis was huge. Klawisz aimed straight forward and took his chance. He fired.

The entire area lit up for a split second as the slug left the gun and traveled the full length of the empty hallway. Klawisz's eyes widened, and he blinked. There had been a Giant Mantis in the hallway, right?

Why was it empty now?

He dared a step, his light shining. Silence. Klawisz heard nothing as he moved but his own heartbeat and footsteps on the carpet. No Mantis. No noise. No nothing. He kept moving forward gun straight ahead until he reached the glowing vending machines. The elevator gate was closed, and the cables unmoving.

Klawisz lowered the gun an inch. "Where did you go?"

The attack came from above.

The swipe of the curved forelimb, jutted down from the ceiling and latched onto Klawisz's shoulder. He yelled as the blade of it cut into his coat, slicing straight through the shirt and flesh. The gush of blood bubbled up under the fabric and he twisted until the flashlight shown at the ceiling, lighting up the giant eyes.

Klawisz swung the shotgun up and fired, spraying the thing smack in the face with the slug.

The head popped off like a champagne cork, with a sickening crack and the deafening fire of the gun. Klawisz stumbled back as the body dropped from the ceiling. The limbs twitched, flailing in the air as the body continued moving without a head. Klawisz scrambled back, his arm throbbing with pain as he scooted back and dug through his pockets for the last of his ammunition.

The scimitar-like forelimb slammed into the ground between his legs and the other hit on his right side. Klawisz pulled his leg up and rolled, smacking into the side of a locked door. He cracked the gun open, hands trembling as he shoved the next two rounds into the gun. His last two rounds.

The Headless Mantis continued thrashing its limbs, up and down, aiming for something it couldn't see. The side of the upper arm smacked into Klawisz as he crawled to his feet, slamming him into the side wall of the corridor. He cried out as the wounded shoulder smashed into the wall, leaving a thick trail of dark blood. Klawisz pushed off the wall and shoved the end of the shotgun into the joint where the thorax met its pulsing, fat abdomen.

He fired.

Split in two, the Mantis stopped moving, save for a twitch of the legs. Klawisz backed away from the corpse, tripping over the front arm as he went. He fell on his back, and knocked the gun hard enough that it misfired, sending his last remaining shot through the nearest door on the other side of the hallway.

Klawisz stayed down on his side, hugging the warm gun and catching his breath. Hot blood soaked and seeped through his clothes from his shoulder, and he reached an arm up to shove the fabric of his coat into the wound.

He needed to wrap that.

Klawisz struggled to his feet, using the gun as a crutch. He kicked the dead Mantis for good measure before looking at the door he'd shot. Klawisz reached in his jean pocket for his room key, and pulled it out. He set it in the the lock; it didn't move. Not a match. Tired and aching, Klawisz stuck his hand through the hole in the door, and unlocked it from the inside with a solid click.

The light in the room was broken, but Klawisz's flashlight still worked. The beam spreading farther in the room than in the hallway, it landed on the bed. Klawisz dropped his shotgun on the floor and leaned it against the wall as he stumbled forward toward the waiting medical kit on the bedspread.

CHAPTER 14

KLAWISZ HELD HIS coat over his arm, his shoulder freshly wrapped and cleaned using the first aid kit he'd found on the bed in the room. With the dead body of the Mantis, the atmosphere on the floor had grown sweltering and humid. Klawisz had sweat beading on his brows and soaking his shirt.

He dragged the shotgun along behind him as he finished his round in the dark hallway. Each door checked, and each not a match. Klawisz stumbled over the body of the dead Mantis again in the dark, and cursed its existence with every foul word he knew in English and Polish.

None of them felt appropriate enough to fully express his hatred.

Satisfied and out of breath, Klawisz tugged his peacoat back on, leaving it unbuttoned on the front. He wandered to the remaining stairwell door, the one on the other side still disappeared into the void somehow. He could't shoot the knob off the door, but he could get it open. While not as good as the crowbar or the ax, Klawisz found the end of the shotgun worked as a decent club. He raised it and slammed it against the door knob.

Over and over.

Until sweat flew from his face, and his shoulder burned in agony, Klawisz hit the door knob with the butt of the gun.

It snapped off after the fifteen hit, when his arms burned and his back ached.

Klawisz pushed open the door, and stepped onto the concrete landing. He rested his weight on the stairwell rail, and tugged himself along and up. The metal railing creaked under his weight, but he kept going up. The midpoint landing was a welcome sight, and has he rounded the corner, Klawisz stopped.

His hand shook on the railing.

"No," Klawisz said. He pushed on, climbing up the four or five steps that he could before his head was an inch from the out of place concrete barrier. He pressed his palm flat on the low ceiling that cut into the stairs and shouted, "No!"

The path to the thirteenth floor door had been cut off.

"No," Klawisz repeated. He turned and tore down the steps, ignoring the shifting of his bandages under his coat. He ignored the fresh stream of blood as it came free from the loosened bandages and continued tearing down the stairs. "No, no, no!"

Klawisz passed by the twelfth floor and stopped at the eleventh. He kicked open the door with more force than he knew he could contain, shattering the lock as it burst open. Klawisz ran down the hallway, arms at his sides. He stopped only once when his maps flew out of his pockets from the speed. Klawisz cursed, gathering them all back up, his palms wet and every inch of him in agony and pain from the hunger and the wound.

He buttoned his coat pocket up to keep from losing his things again and kept going.

Through the already broken door on the other side and up the stairs he went, once again passing by the wretched dark twelfth floor. He kept going up until he was met with the same concrete barrier as the other side in the same place.

Klawisz heaved a heavy breath, salty tears mixing with his sweat as he pressed both palms on the ceiling. He pushed up, hoping to move the barrier and give him back his path to the last floor of the building.

He dropped his head, staring at the concrete steps. Klawisz's nails scratched along the rough grey surface of the ceiling blocking his way, scraping off the skin of his fingertips. "I just want to go to my room."

CHAPTER 15

KLAWISZ SAT DEFEATED on the carpet floor of the third floor hallway.

He'd kept his hand pressed against the concrete barrier between the twelfth floor and the thirteenth for near an hour before time caught up with him again.

With nothing else to do, he tugged his leather journal from his pocket, wincing at the stains of blood that had seeped into the pages. The splotches covered his drawings and notes, but he read through them all the same. Looking for anything he may have missed. That he could check again. His notes held no answers, only reminders of things he'd already seen.

"Things change a lot around here," Bell had said.

Holding to that hope, he drew one hateful doodle of the Mantis on the twelfth floor and closed the journal. Something had to have changed. He must have missed the path to the last floor. Klawisz stumbled down the steps, already prepared to start his search over from scratch.

He checked all the floors he could reach again, save for the sixth, which was still on fire.

There was a point he had even checked the lobby, trying his key on the doors just off to the side near the staff areas. Just in some hope that his room might of been in an odd place. When the Concierge had came to tell him to stop, materializing even without the call of his service bell, Klawisz decked him across the face.

The man had hit the ground with a thud, and Klawisz watched silently as Bell came running to check on his master.

"You're a menace, Mr. Wiśniowski," the Concierge had said as Bell helped him to his feet and away from the filthy floor. He snarled, slicking his hair back and cursing Klawisz's existence with his eyes and the twist of his lips. "I can't remember the last time we had such a troubled guest in our midst. We've been nothing but courteous and this is how you repay us."

"Courtesy would be telling me where my room is," Klawisz responded, holding up his key by the scratched fob. His voice sounded angry and dull at the same time in his own ears, as if it couldn't make up its mind. "All I want is to go to my room."

"So you've said, over and over like a broken record," the Concierge said. He straightened his suit and shook his head. "For all our sakes, I hope you find it soon."

Bell had walked up to Klawisz's side after the Concierge left and opened his mouth like he wanted to say something. He was cut off as the Concierge shouted, "Bell!" across the room. The bellboy flinched and ran away from Klawisz and back to his position on the wall to wait for luggage that was never going to show up.

When it was clear no more would be said, Klawisz had retreated back to the stairwell and left them both.

He started his search again.

Every floor he'd checked. Every nook and every cranny of this building from braving the Scorpion to breaking down the doors with his ax. The crowbar. His boot. His key. None of them leading to where he wanted to go.

An empty shell, Klawisz stared at the tips of his boots.

He stayed that way until a second pair of shoes entered his vision, polished and part of a uniform he'd come to know quite intimately. Klawisz looked up and saw the universe in a pair of concerned, caring eyes. No mockery on his face, no pity. Only care and concern. The elevator operator knelt, resting his arm on his knee. His starry eyes kept Klawisz's own locked.

"There's still one floor you've yet to check, Mr. Wiśniowski," Dashiell said. He gestured behind him to the waiting elevator behind the rusted gates. "And there's only one way to get there."

Klawisz shook his head. "No, not the elevator. Been in it once. It's a death trap."

"It's quite safe," Dashiell said, soothing and slow. "You passed out last time from hunger, not the elevator."

"You said you didn't know where my room was," Klawisz accused.

"I don't," Dashiell said, "but I do know there's only one place you haven't looked and I'd be more than happy to take you there."

"No," Klawisz said, his chest heaving and the tears gathering in the corner of his eyes. "Can't."

"You are a delightfully stubborn man, Mr. Wiśniowski. It is my duty and privilege to take the best of care of our guests, which has always included you," Dashiell said. "So perhaps just this once, why don't you do me the honor of a little trust, and allow me to assist you?"

Dashiell held out his hand, the palm open and inviting. He waited, patient.

Klawisz stared down the elevator, his chest heaving. Dashiell was right. There was only one place he hadn't checked. No matter how his stomach turned at the thought of taking up the offer. Dashiell waited patiently, kneeling even now, unmoving and trusting that Klawisz would allow him to do his job.

What the hell?

He took the offered hand, and allowed Dashiell to pull him to his feet.

The threshold of the elevator loomed like a threatening lion's mouth ready to swallow Klawisz whole as his toes touched the edge of it. He swallowed, and with Dashiell patiently waiting inside with his hand on the control, Klawisz took his first willing step into the elevator car.

The entirely of the car sunk an inch with Klawisz's added weight and he sucked in a heavy breath in time with the rusted and clean steel gates both closing behind him in tandem.

"I'm so happy that you've finally come around," Dashiell said, slamming the control switch all the way down so that the arrow on the other end landed on the brilliant number thirteen. "I'll be sure to tell Bell you changed your mind. There was a bet going."

"Lucky Bell," Klawisz said, swaying as the car began its upward climb. He clung to the hand railings and rested his forehead against the wall of the car. His fingers sweat and he rested there. "Or lucky you?"

"Neither," Dashiell said, his voice oddly warm. Klawisz didn't need to turn to see his smile. "It wasn't that sort of bet."

Klawisz listened to the stretch of the cable as the car moved, his body heavy and limp as it rocked and swayed on its long climb up the building.

He could practically hear the manual pumps below struggling as they carried the car the full way up the elevator shaft. Klawisz turned and placed his back against the wall and closed his eyes.

"I must say though," Dashiell said, "if you don't mind me speaking out of turn, that is?"

"Go ahead," Klawisz said. *Not that it's stopped you before,* he thought to himself.

"It has been quite the delight being able to serve you, Mr. Wiśniowski. It's not often we get guests who are as stubborn, hardheaded and all around as entertaining as you are," Dashiell said. Klawisz opened his eyes, listening to the wistful tone as Dashiell continued speaking. His voice acting as though he were longing for older times; something nostalgic. "And it's most certainly not often that we get to spend so much time with a guest. I do believe you made both Annie and Julie's nights to have an actual customer to serve. Even Bell has seemed more chipper, and I'd be lying if I said I haven't grown quite fond of you myself."

"Could have fooled me," Klawisz said.

"I'm sure we could have," Dashiell chuckled. "But even if you did raise the Concierge's blood pressure a few notches, I'm sure even he'll be sorry to see you retire."

Klawisz rubbed his face, and listened to the moving elevator. "Somehow I doubt that."

"It's quite true," Dashiell said, insistent. "You've kept all of us on our toes."

"Must be boring around here with only one guy to make bets on," Klawisz said, rubbing the side of his cheek.

"One?" Dashiell asked, lifting an eyebrow and laughing. "Odd thing to say considering you've met some of our other guests while on your little rampage through the hotel."

Klawisz turned toward Dashiell, dropping his hand down to his chest. His hand found his journal through the coat fabric, hiding away in his pocket. "What?"

"Granted, considering how much you seemed to hate them, I'm not surprised you don't count them as people like yourself," Dashiell said. He hummed, licking the side of his lips. "As much as we dedicate ourselves to perfect service, rules say we can't interfere with guests interacting with guests no matter how bloody it gets.

"Unless of course you're stealing from their rooms," Dashiell said.

"Then we get to take a step in, as I'm sure you noticed when the Concierge confiscated a bit of your stolen things. Rooms are sacred, you know. The one place where a guest's privacy is to be respected and protected. It's no wonder you've seen so much of us, considering all the breaking and entering you've insisted upon."

"I met other guests?" Klawisz asked himself, his gut churning.

"You did," Dashiell said, watching Klawisz with those knowing eyes. A shooting star flew past the bed of twinkling lights, acting like a wink. "I wouldn't think too much on it. You're hardly the first, and will not be the last, to draw blood around this place."

The only other living things he'd seen in this hotel were the staff and the monster insects. He'd met a corpse and some ghosts, but other than employees, there hadn't been any other human guests. Klawisz was the only one. The rooms had all been empty.

He shook his head as flashes of the various Insects he'd run across entered his mind. His hand clutched his journal through his coat. Couldn't be. Klawisz' stomach twisted as he thought of the ones he'd *killed*. Dashiell was crazy. Had to be crazy.

"Regardless," Dashiell said, humming lightly. "What I said earlier is true: It has been a treat having you here with us, Mr. Wiśniowski."

The conversation grew quiet after that, as Klawisz leaned his head against the side wall of the car. He covered his face with his hands and breathed in. His shoulder ached. His stomach growled. And Dashiell's breathing filled the car with sound so that Klawisz could concentrate on anything else other than his own beating heart.

The car rocked and came to an abrupt halt.

Klawisz stared at the number at the top of the car and saw the tiny light had stopped on thirteen. "Here already?"

"Time moves quickly when your thoughts are alive," Dashiell said. He reached forward and pulled open the gates. He held his hand out, allowing Klawisz to exit the car. "After you, sir."

He stepped foot out of the car, and shook his head. He turned back around to Dashiell and said, "There must be some mistake."

"No, I do believe you're in the right place," Dashiell said, closing the gate. He smiled warmly, his eyes still alive as ever, filled with brilliant stars on a bed of the universe. Dashiell bowed at the waist, and took hold of the control. "It was my utmost pleasure to escort you, Klawisz. I do hope to see you again, and I can only imagine just how amazing you'll be the next time I have the pleasure. Until then, please have a pleasant night."

Klawisz watched as the elevator descended down the shaft, leaving him alone in the small penthouse floor lobby.

CHAPTER 16

THE ONE DOOR loomed just behind Klawsiz's back as he continued staring at the empty elevator shaft, scared to turn around and face it. The once terrifying gaping hole now seemed a hundred times more appealing than the doorway that was behind him. There was only one room on the thirteen floor: the penthouse.

All this time.

Klawisz turned around, ignoring the clean and perfect condition of the small lobby. A welcome mat waited for him in front of the door, potted plants decorating each side of the cleanly painted doorframe. The number plaques had long fallen off, the nails that once held the embossed letters still in place.

The room key burned a hole in Klawisz's pocket. His hand squeezed tight around it as the air lodged in Klawisz's throat. He pulled the key from its fabric pocket prison, and caressed it in his palm.

He held his key, holding the fob up next to the door. Embedded in the door, was a set of scratches that matched the ones on his key fob. They were identical in every way, and it made Klawisz want to sob at the promise that held.

It took two steps to reach the door.

His fingers trembled as they wrapped around the key, and held the teeth of it near the doorknob.

Klawisz inserted the key, slowly and listening for each miniature piston to dance over the key's teeth as he pressed it all the way in. He held his breath, and turned the key. The knob followed with it, and Klawisz heard the *click* of the door unlocking.

He rested his head against the door and grabbed the doorknob with the full of his hand. He twisted and threw the door open, revealing his room.

The penthouse sitting room awaited him, cleaned and ready for its owner to come home. Klawisz stumbled through the doorway, leaving the key in the lock and his hand slipping off the knob. A small table was a few paces in front of him, holding a phone and a small set of hotel stationary with a complimentary pen. A stack of papers sat on the side, and Klawisz dared to look:

His room bill.

Klawisz laughed hysterically has he flipped through page after page of charges. Every bit of vandalism from the first broken door on the main floor to the ones he'd taken down with the shotgun. All individually listed with a time, date, and charges owed for their repair.

There was even a side list for services rendered due to his behavior, such as crowbar proof security and therapy for the Scorpion.

Klawisz threw the stack of papers back onto the table and continued through the room. There was only one place he wanted to be right now. Only one place that would make him complete.

The bedroom door of the suite was just off to the left of the sitting area. He had forgotten everything when he was wandering around the hotel, but with each step it all came back to him. Memories of the layout, and where each and every piece of furniture in this suite was laid out. His feet knew where to go, and he stomped there in his boots, his hand reaching for the bedroom door. Klawisz found the knob and his hand turned and—

The bedroom door was locked.

The laugh was lost in a choke at the base of his throat, and Klawisz felt the tears pouring down the side of his face. Of course it was. He growled and felt no shame slamming his shoulder into the side of the door. What was one more damage charge after the time he'd had?

The door, as if feeling his mood, gave way easily to the assault and opened without trouble. Klawisz stumbled through the doorway like a drunkard, his eyes already falling on him and the sweet promise of clean sheets and bedding far outweighing any other.

The king size bed waited for him, as if it knew Klawisz was calling.

He found a buttercream mint on the pillow, along with a "Welcome" card. Klawisz ate the mint, and fell spread eagle on his back onto the top of the bed's comforter. He lay there unmoving in his peacoat, his knees bent on the edge of the bed with his boots dangling just above the floor. It felt like falling into a dream, the softness of the mattress under his back as his body sunk into his bed.

Klawisz closed his eyes, and breathed in deep.

He heard the front door of the suite close; a deafening and loud echoing sound signifying the end of something. He sunk further into the mattress, uncaring and without worry. This was how it was supposed to be. Something deep and stirring in his soul said it to be true.

Klawisz fell asleep to the click of a locked door.

Acknowledgements

To God be the glory forever, and ever, Amen.

As always: Thanks to God in the highest for the talent to write, and the push He gave to everyone who inspired me, helped me, and encouraged me. And of course, thanks be to God for giving us Jesus, who loves you & me.

At this particular moment: I want to give a big shout and thanks to the Horror Video Game Industry. The writers, programers, coders, testers, players, and everyone else involved in the process to bring us some of the best, scariest, and most entertaining Video Games out there. You've told some amazing stories, created some fantastic scares, and I really love everyone involved. Keep it up!

And of course, I always need to drop in an extra thank you for the friends and family to continue to support me in my writing endeavors, as well as the readers who continue to make my day with every book they choose to pick up! Thank you so much.

About The Author

Grey Liliy is a young woman who claims the East Coast of Virginia as her home. She enjoys anime, video games, movies, novels, and comics of just about any genre. Liliy has been drawing & writing a comic of her own since 2005, called *The Adventures of Wiglaf and Mordred*. Her debut novel, *Children of Hephaestus* was published in September 2012.

www.ingramcontent.com/pod-product-compliance
Lightning Source LLC
Chambersburg PA
CBHW052142220626
47052CB00005B/1161